Fated Mates Series

Volume One

Leanora Moore

Other Novels by Leanora Moore:

- The Caress of a Younger Man
- Heavenly Kingdom

The Voluptuously Curvy and Loving It Series:

- Smooth as Silk
- Finding Love Within
- His Forgotten Lover
- Drafted for Love
- Planning for Forever

Musical Curves Series:

- Rhymes from Heart
- Producing Love Together
- Composing Her Desires

Acknowledgement

First and foremost, I must thank God, because without him, I wouldn't have the gift to tell my stories. God has brought me through a lot of things in my life and I know it was only by his grace and mercy.

Secondly, I want to thank my family, for being so supportive and pushing me to keep going. My kids are my reason for living and they give me a reason to keep writing and to better myself. I must thank Justin Cowan, because without him pushing me to finish this book, it never would have been done this soon.

Lastly, I must thank my fans, because you guys have supported me for almost nine years and are still going strong. I enjoy the emails I get from you, encouraging me to keep writing and how my writing touches you and influences your life. I promise you all that I will continue to give you my best work and I have a lot more stories coming out soon.

By Leanora Moore

Alpha I Need You

A Werewolf Love Story

Chapter One

Rachel's POV:

"I'm so sick of these damn rogues, how many in our pack were injured?" I ask Lamont Jackson, my beta and best friend while trying to control my wolf. As the Alpha of the pack, I take the welfare of my pack very serious.

"Rachel, we only have three warriors with minor injuries. We were lucky that our patrol team warned us about the rogues being in the area," Lamont replied as Shannon, his mate and my younger sister walked into my office after knocking on my door.

Looking at my baby sister, "Shannon, what can I do for you?" I asked her because she knew not to interrupt my meetings.

Coming to stand in front of my desk, "I wanted to let you know that we've tended to the wounded and everyone has eaten and headed to bed," she replied before she looked over at her mate.

Nodding my head, "Thank you for all your help, is there anything else?" I asked when I saw her and my beta looking at each other nervously.

Taking a deep breath, "Actually, we wanted to tell you something, but then the attack happened. So, we didn't get a chance," Lamont replied as he grabbed Shannon's hand and smiled at her.

Sighing, "Alright, the suspense is killing me! Just tell me already," I yelled. Can you tell I don't like playing the guessing games? My sister uses to do that a lot when we were kids. Making me play twenty questions before getting to the point.

"First, promise you won't get mad and overreact," Shannon suggested as she stepped closer to Lamont, as he put his arm around her shoulders and kissed her forehead.

My only reply was to put my elbows on my custom-made mahogany wood desk and put my face in my hands and growl.

Now as you may have guessed, I'm Rachel Manning and the oldest sibling of my family. I just turned eighteen and took my place as Alpha after our parents, the previous Alpha and Luna, Thomas and Kelly Manning stepped down. They decided to do some traveling, now that I took my rightful place as Alpha. Which was how I found myself stuck babysitting my sixteen-year-old sister, who just found her mate just a few months ago after she changed into her wolf for the first time. Now I feel a little uncomfortable because her mate happens to be my best friend and beta. So, you can see the problems I'm facing. Plus, I must adjust to being an alpha for a pack, called the Yellowstone Pack with about 350 members and making sure everything runs smoothly. Luckily, we are based in Colorado, which is known for its wooded areas in the mountains, so we don't have to worry about humans venturing into our area much. Recently, we've had issues with rogues and it's starting to get out of hand.

Looking up, "Shannon, you and Lamont have two seconds to tell me what's going on," I demanded before pushing back from my desk and standing up. I don't have time for my sister's guessing games when I must hunt down rogues and look after my pack.

"Rachel, we just found out that we're having a pup in five months and we wanted your permission to get married as soon as possible," Lamont replied looking me in my eyes, then looked at the floor to show his respect to me as his Alpha. When a female wolf becomes pregnant, the pregnancy only runs for six months instead of nine, which makes my sister a month into her pregnancy.

All I could do was sit back down because it was like a million emotions hit me all at once, as I closed my eyes and rubbed my forehead as a migraine developed. Yes, I was pissed that my baby sister got pregnant at sixteen and hadn't finished high school yet. I was also happy for her, because she had a wonderful mate to start her family with, and I knew that he would be there for her. Then I guess you could say I was a like jealous that I was eighteen years old, with a ton of responsibilities, and to make it even worse, I still hadn't found my mate. I knew he was out there, and I hoped I found him soon because lately I felt like half of me was missing.

"Sis, we love each other very much, and I know I disappointed you, but please don't be mad at me," my sister said as tears ran down her face. Seeing her cry brought me out of my emotions and made me really look at my sister and realize she's not the same little girl that use to follow me around all the time.

"Rachel, you know I love your sister, and I will do everything in my power to make her happy," Lamont added as he hugged my sister who was still crying.

Sighing, "Lamont, if I didn't believe that you would make sure my baby sister was happy, I would've pulled your balls through your throat," I stated as I stood up and walked around my desk before I stood in front of the couple.

As I looked at my sister again, I could see that she had grown up and that she truly loved Lamont and their pup, "Shannon, yes, I'm upset that you didn't wait until you were older and out of school, but you are still my sister and I love you. As for my permission for you two to get married, you have it as long as I can be your maid of honor," I said before I pulled her into my arms and hugged her.

"Of course, you're my maid of honor, my sister and my best friend," Shannon replied as she hugged me back.

Stepping back and smiling at the happy couple, "Alright, you two go and start planning your wedding, while I finish going over all this paperwork and arrangements for the meeting we're having here next week with the all the Alphas in this area, to talk about the rogue attacks," I suggested as I pushed them out my office door.

Smiling, "Alright, and thanks for believing in us. If you need me, just let me know. I also put all the reports on your desk and made arrangements for the Alphas to stay in the West Wing of the packhouse," Lamont stated as he grabbed Shannon's hand and pulled her into his arms. Seeing them together gave me hope that I would find my mate and experience the happiness that they share together.

"Alright, see you two later," I replied before I shut my office door and walked back to my desk.

Sitting behind my desk, looking at the list of Alphas attending the area meeting and ran across a name I hadn't seen since I was fourteen years old. Damon Jackson was the boy of every girl's dream when they were growing up, with skin the color of smooth caramel, hair in soft dreads and paired with the prettiest emerald-green eyes I had ever seen. Last time I had heard anything about him, he was traveling the world looking for his mate. Which means, he must have found her, if he was home and now was the Alpha of the Jade Pack, which happened to be our neighboring pack. I remember the day he left, and I also remember how we hugged each other while promising to stay in touch. After he left I cried myself to sleep many nights because we were close, and I felt like I had lost one of my closest friends. I hope he found his mate because Damon was the sweetest person I have ever known.

After looking over the arrangements and reports, I decided to grab something to eat and head to bed, when Lamont busted into my office causing me to get into a defensive stance.

"Rachel, we have a problem!"

Chapter Two

Damon's POV:

Looking at the cards in my hand, "Man, why the hell can't I find my mate?" I asked my best friends.

As usual, my friends and I got together for poker night since it was Friday. It was usually Joshua Daniels, who was my beta, and then there is Ben Kelly, David Anthony, Ty Smith, and Andrew Lewis, who are my strongest fighters and trackers. We've all been friends since we were pups, and we trust each other with our lives.

"Damon, you will find her when the goddess wants you to," Joshua replied sitting across the dining room table from me.

"We will find our mates, we just have to be patient," Ty suggested as he threw his cards on the table.

Smiling, "Plus, we have that meeting coming next week, maybe you will meet them there," David added while throwing his cards down too.

Shaking my head, "Man, I hear what you all are saying, but I've been searching for my mate for years," I replied as I laid my royal flush on the table, causing everyone to lay their cards down. As I pulled the winning pot towards me, I thought about the upcoming meeting and realized I would get to see Rachel Manning again after so many years, since her pack was hosting it. I hadn't really had time to think about her or anything else in the last couple of months. I had only been home a few months before taking the Alpha position from my dad after he stepped down. I really hadn't had much time to think about anything else but my pack, especially with the rogue attacks in the area.

When I left home to search for my mate, it felt like I was leaving a piece of my heart. When I left her standing on her front porch with tears in her eyes the last day I was home, I thought about not leaving at all, but I knew I needed to find my mate.

"It's good to see that you can still kick our butts at poker," Joshua joked causing all of us to laugh.

"Man, you know that I always kick your butts," I replied as I leaned back into my chair. My buddies suck at poker, but we always enjoyed our guy time, plus it helped us release some stress.

Looking around the table, "Speaking of the meeting, has anyone seen Rachel since we've been home?" I asked as I watched the guys pause and then look at each other. We all grew up together with Rachel and her pack, plus all our parents were close friends. At that moment my parents and Rachel's were traveling the world after they had passed the packs down to us. I know I sound like a bad friend, and I should've gone and seen Rachel myself, but I've been so busy with all the recent rogue attacks. So, I had to focus on my pack and keep them safe.

"No, I haven't! With everything going on, I was waiting until the meeting since we are staying with her for a few days," Andrew replied as just before the other guys said no also.

As the guys talked, I thought about all the times Rachel and I spent at each other's houses, and the big crush I had on her growing up. She reminded me of an angel, with her naturally curly hair that fell to the middle of her back, her smooth caramel skin and her body even as a teenager made a boy say amen. I mean, she had perky breast that could fill my hand perfectly, which I had felt while pretending to tickle her. Rachel's best feature was her gray eyes. When she looked at you, it was as if she could see into your soul.

"Man, are you going to play or sit there daydreaming?" Joshua asked as he finished dealing, and I looked around the table and the guys were all smirking at me.

"I thought you were tired of getting your butts whipped, but I can play one more hand," I joked as I picked up my hand and put it in order. When I looked around the table I could tell by their facial expressions that they didn't have shit.

Just as we put our bets on the table "Alpha, the rogues are attacking the Yellowstone Pack on our east borderline," Devin shouted through our pack link. I had Devin and three others who were good at tracking and fighting patrol our border for rogues.

"We're on the way," I shouted as the guys, some other pack members, and myself all ran out the front door of the packhouse and I shifted into my all black wolf in midair and took off running. I can never get over the feeling of coming alive when I shift into my wolf. All my senses were intensified, and I feel a stronger connection with my pack.

As we arrived on the scene, we found an all-out war going on. Devin and our other patrollers along with the Yellowstone pack were fighting the rogues, which you could tell who they were by their smell and their red eyes that seemed so full of hate. Seeing that more rogues were about to join the party, we ran to help the Yellowstone pack. Seeing Kathy, one of my best fighters getting cornered by three rogues, I ran and jumped on the biggest one in the middle. I grabbed his neck in my mouth and bit down until I heard a sickening snap, and then I threw his limp body on the ground. Looking around me, I saw that Devin, Kathy's mate, and Kathy had taken care of the other two.

Looking around I saw that everyone was still fighting, and when I looked to my left I saw the prettiest white wolf with black on her paws and the tips of her ears being cornered by two big rogues that were bigger than the rest.

Just as I was about to help her, a rogue jumped on my back, biting into my shoulder, rolling over I was able to shack him off me. Then as we began circling each other, I waited for him to attack first and when he jumped in the air, I jumped up and with my paw, I hit him in the jaw with all my strength and I heard a loud snap as he head swung to the left and his body fell to the ground. Looking around I saw the white wolf was still fighting the two rogues, so I ran and jumped on the back of the one on the right side. Biting into the back of his neck and as I tried to snap his neck, he rolled over making me lose my grip. Soon as we both stood up, he jumped at me, but I was able to hit him in the face with my paw and as he fell to the ground, I pounced on him and ripped out his throat. After his body went limp, I looked to my left and saw the white wolf finish off her opponent. Taking a deep breath and looking around, I saw that the rogues were either dead or retreating into the woods.

After walking around to make sure everyone was alright, we only had minor injuries to deal with. Seeing that the rogues were gone, we all shifted back to our human bodies, so we could pile up the rogues' bodies and burn them. After putting on a pair of gym shorts that Andrew had tossed me, I was about to pick up a dead rogue when I looked to my left, and saw the white wolf transform into the most beautiful woman I had ever seen, and when I looked into her eyes, it was like someone had punched me in my gut. She had the most stunning gray eyes, and then I realized I only knew one woman with those eyes, and my wolf was going crazy, wanting to go to her and hold her.

"Rachel!" I shouted as I walked toward her, and when she looked at me, her eyes grew wide as a smile formed on her lips.

"Damon!" she shouted as she ran toward me. We met in the middle of the field and ran into each other's arms.

Feeling her amazing body in my arms, it felt as if she was made for me, as sparks shot throughout my body, and when I pulled back from her, she had the same shocked expression on her face that I'm sure was on mine. Then she smacked my face.

"What the hell?" I yelled as I rubbed my cheek.

Chapter Three

Rachel's POV:

"You lied to me, and then you have the nerve to come here as if nothing is wrong," I yelled as rage rushed through my body.

Seeing Damon again opened a lot of old wounds I had, but that didn't stop me from noticing that he was still fine as hell. He still had the effect on me that when we touched, I would feel electricity shoot through my entire body. I saw that he still had those hypnotic emerald-green eyes, and lord have mercy, that guy had a body that would make any woman weak at the knees.

"Rachel, what the hell are you talking about?" Damon asked drawing me from my thoughts, and as I looked around, I realized Joshua, and the other guys I grew up with from Damon's pack was walking toward us along with my pack.

Clearing my throat, "Damon, let's take this to the packhouse," I whispered as our packs crowded around us. Then I turned to his best friends smiling, "Long time no see."

Smiling, "I'm scared to hug you, you may slap us too," Joshua joked before we hugged, causing us all to laugh. Then I heard a low growl and when I turned around I realized it was Damon.

Shaking my head, "No, I save those for Damon," I replied as I hugged the other guys and then grinned at Damon, who had an intense look on his face.

"Well, take it easy on him, he's had a hard time lately," Ty whispered in my ear as Damon and I stared at each other. As we stared at each other, it was like he was pulling me to him, and my body felt like it was on fire with desire.

"Mate! Go to him!" my inner wolf, Lisa screamed.

"What!" I replied to her in my head.

"He's our mate dummy," she replied before laughing at me.

As you can tell, my inner wolf was a mess. She could be cranky one minute and playful the next, but don't piss us off, because she would take over in a heartbeat and rip out your throat.

Shaking my head, "I can't be his mate! Plus, He has already found his mate, and that's why he came home," I told my wolf as my heart rate increased and my palms became sweaty. We both whimpered at the thought of Damon being with another woman.

"Rachel, are you alright?" Lamont asked me, bringing me out of our trance. After looking over at him, I looked around us to see our packs staring at me.

Sighing, "Yeah, I'm fine. Did we have any serious injuries?" I asked going into Alpha mode because at that moment my thoughts were everywhere, and I had to keep myself from jumping Damon's bones in front of everyone. The mating bond I have with him was getting strong by the minute and the desire was almost unbearable.

"We're all fine, and we took care of the bodies," Lamont replied looking between me and Damon with a smirk on his face.

As you can tell, everyone knew about me and Damon's close relationship before he left. Just to give you an example of how close we were, we have known each other since we were pups, then as we got older we were inseparable. We were either at his house or mine, plus we had clothes at each other's house. Seeing him now, I realized how much I missed him, and now I find out he's my mate. Can my life get any more complicated?

Taking a deep breath to calm my racing heart, "Alright, what are you guys doing in my neck of the woods?" I asked Damon and the guys, and when I looked into his eyes, it was as if he was undressing me with his eyes.

"I had my scouts patrolling our borders and they reported that they saw rogues attacking you, so we came to help out," Damon replied and his pack nodded their heads in agreement.

"Thank you, guys! It seemed like they were coming from every direction," I stated remembering how surprised I was to see about 30 to 40 rogues, then I started to wonder why they keep attacking my pack.

"It's strange that they keep attacking us," Lamont added, voicing my concern.

"Do you have anyone that would want to harm you or your pack?" Andrew asked looking at me and Lamont.

Shaking his head, "Not that I know of," Lamont replied then he looked at me.

As soon as Andrew asked us that question, a chill ran down my spine and I began to remember the worst night of my life, that I had never told anyone about. I still had nightmares about that terrible night. As the night in question ran through my mind, I remembered the last thing that the guy told me before I ran away.

"I will make you pay!" he yelled at me.

Shaking my head to get rid of the memory, "No, it can't be!" as my heart rate started racing.

Chapter Four

Damon's POV:

"Mate, something's wrong with our mate," My wolf Joseph screamed as I looked at Rachel and her face became pale and her hands started shaking.

At first, I was shocked that my mate turned out to be my childhood friend, but then my instincts kicked in and I had to have her in my arms.

Walking over to her "Rachel, what is wrong? You're shaking like a leaf," I asked before taking her into my arms.

Now don't get me wrong, feeling her soft and sexy body next to mine was making my wolf go crazy, even though he was worried something was wrong with her.

"Rachel are you alright?" Lamont said as our packs surrounded us.

Taking a deep breath, "Lamont, there is something we need to discuss, I just need some time to get my head together first. Let's head back to our packhouse and we can discuss everything," Rachel replied and then she looked up at me.

Turning to look at their pack, "Alright, everyone let's head back," Lamont commanded, and they all shifted and headed home leaving Lamont, Rachel, Me, and my pack.

Looking at my pack, "Alright everyone, thank you for helping and you can head back," I said, and they all shifted and after bowing their head to me they disappeared into the woods.

"Damon, thank you for helping us, and if you don't mind would you and the guy's mind coming with us, this concerns all the packs in the area, so you may as well hear this also," Rachel suggested as she pulled herself out of my arms. I instantly wanted to pull her back to me, but I knew that she was in alpha mode and whatever she needed to say was important.

Nodding my head, "Sure Rachel, you know we got your back," I replied smiling at her.

I just wanted five minutes alone with her, so we could talk.

"Rachel, you're like our little sister, so you know if you need anything you just have to ask," Ty added while putting an arm around her shoulder. That instantly made my wolf go crazy and causing me to release a growl, making everyone look at me like I was crazy.

"Damon are you alright?" Joshua asked me through our pack mind link.

"Yeah Man, you sounded like you were going to ripe Ty apart," Ben added also in my head.

"You wouldn't believe me if I told you," I replied as the rest of our group started talking and Joshua looked at me.

"Try me," they all replied with a smirk on their faces, and as you could tell we really were close and knew every little crazy thing about each other.

"Are you guys ready to leave?" Rachel asked looking at us, and I had the urge to kiss that sad look of her face.

"Yeah, we're ready! Lead the way," I said as we turned and followed Lamont and her.

"After all the searching I've done, I found my mate. The crazy thing is that I've known her my whole life," I confessed in the mind link as I shook my head as we continued following Rachel and Lamont as they are talking about something.

"Are you telling us that Rachel is your mate?" David asked looking at me.

"D, you've got to be joking," Andrew said as we came to the clearing where we could see their packhouse.

"Do you think she knows?" Joshua asked as we continued to walk, and we caught up the Rachel and Lamont.

"I don't know, but I will find out tonight. I've spent the past five years searching for her and I'm not wasting any more time," I replied feeling like I needed to be with her at all times. I hate feeling like something was missing from my life and since I found her, I finally feel complete and

I'm not going to lose her again. So, I needed to find out what had her so scared.

As we walked up to the front door of their packhouse, we saw a box with an envelope sitting on the porch step. Rachel was the first one to the porch and grabbed the box.

"I wonder who left this," Rachel said as she opened the box, and as soon as she had the box opened, she started shaking again and dropped the box.

When the box hits the ground, spilling its contents, we saw that inside the box was a bunch of pictures of Rachel in her bedroom sleeping, coming out of the shower, sitting in her office, and some of her outside walking around.

Trying to contain the growl rumbling in my chest, "Rachel, do you know who sent you these pictures?" I asked as I walked over to her and pulled her into my arms. I was trying to control my wolf from taking over and hunting down whoever was doing that to her.

Sighing, "I have a pretty good idea," She replied as she pulled back and looked into my eyes before she looked at the envelope in her hand.

As she opened the envelope, her hands were visibly shaking, and I understand that she was trying to be brave, but I could see she was about to break down. When she opened the letter and read it, she just handed me the letter and sat down on the porch step as tears ran down her face. Needing to be close her, I sat beside her with my arm around her. I started to read the letter, and as I read it, my wolf screamed to be let loose, and I was tempted to let him.

"Rachel, when did you start dating my cousin?" I asked still in shock.

Chapter Five

Rachel's POV:

Shaking my head "How the fuck did he find me?" was the first thing that entered thoughts when I opened the box seating on my front porch. I felt so violated and scared because he had to be close by to take those pictures. Then I felt someone's arms wrap around me, making me feel safe again, and from the tingles going up my arms, I knew it was Damon.

"Rachel, do you know why he sent you this?" Damon asked me as he pulled me closer to him. Being in his arms almost made me forget all the crazy mess starting to unfold.

"I have a pretty good idea," I replied as I pulled back and looked into his pretty eyes, that I could get lost in for days. Then I looked down at the letter in his clenched fist, and the word from the letter started playing in my mind, but with Damon there somehow, I knew it would be alright.

To My Dearest Rachel,

You've been a bad girl! First, you ruin our last night together, then you left without a trace. Well, I love a good chase and baby I found you. I have enjoyed watching you these past few months, and just know we will be back together soon.

Love u baby,

Eric Jackson

After reading that, I couldn't stand any longer. That's why I handed the letter to Damon and sat down on the porch. As I let my tears flow freely, I felt as if I was releasing all the pain I had hidden from everyone since I came back from college. Then Damon sat beside me and wrapped his arm around me as he read the letter.

"When did you start dating my cousin?" Damon asked, and it was as if someone had thrown a bucket of cold ice water on me.

"Damon, what are you talking about? I met this guy at college, plus I've met all your family and I don't remember ever meeting him," I replied before I stood up after noticing that the guys were starting to crowd around us.

"Guys, why don't we take this inside, especially if we're being watched," Lamont suggested causing me to look over at him.

Nodding my head, "Fine, let's go into my office," I replied as confusion and anger rushed through my body when I thought about someone like Eric trying to control my life.

As we walk in the front door, my sister Shannon was there to greet us.

"Thank the Moon Goddess you're alright," she said as she hugged me and Lamont, and then she noticed Damon and the guys because she started smiling.

Smiling, "We're fine as you can see, thanks to Damon and the guys," I replied, and when I looked at Damon he was staring at me with such intensity that my knees almost buckled.

"Long time no see Damon," Shannon said as she hugged him, causing me to restrain myself from growling at her for touching my mate but it didn't work. I growled anyway making everyone look at me. Instantly Damon was by my side putting his arm around me, instantly calming me down. When I looked up into his eye, they held so much love and understanding that I had to smile. Damn, I still don't get how in the hell, Damon of all people could be my mate. Someone I have loved my whole life, but couldn't have, because I knew he had a mate out there.

"Well if it isn't little Sha Sha all grown up," Andrew jokes breaking the tension in the room as everyone started laughing at her childhood nickname.

Frowning, "You know I hated when you guys call me that," Shannon grumbled as she hugged the guys.

"We knew that! That's why we called you that when you use to follow us around, so you could tell on us. Then you would always run away after you got mad," Ty joked making us all nod our head in agreement as we laughed.

"You all were so mean to me back then," she replied, and Lamont put his arm around her waist that soon will be expanding with my niece or nephew. As you can see, I'm still having a hard time dealing with my baby sister being pregnant at sixteen.

"Rachel, what's wrong?" Shannon asked as she walked up to me, bringing me from my thoughts.

"Nothing, I just have a lot on my mind. Like helping you plan your wedding, and for the new baby," I replied which made her smile.

"Wait a minute! Little Sha Sha is getting married and having a pup?" Joshua asked smiling and making Shannon blush as she walked back to Lamont and put her arms around his waist.

"Yes, we're getting married in a few weeks and having a baby soon," she replied smiling.

Seeing her so happy almost made me forget my drama.

"Congratulations!" the guys cheered at the same time.

Sighing, "Alright, let's head to my office so we can discuss the rogue issue," I suggested then turned and headed to my office.

As I continued to my office, I could feel Damon on my heels. Damon always had a calming presence to me and at that moment I needed it. Opening my door, I walked into my office that was lined with bookshelves and went behind my mahogany desk, where I sat down in my custom-made office chair. While everyone else took a seat on the two sofas sitting around my desk, Damon stood in front of the window with his arms crossed over his bulging chest.

"What's going on?" Shannon asked while looking at me.

"Shannon, this has to do with the rogues that keep attacking us," I replied as I put my elbows on my desk and put my face in my hands before taking a deep breath.

Then when I looked up, everyone's attention was focused on me.

"Alright, what about them?" she asked looking at everyone in the room then back at me.

"I don't even know where to start," I stated hating to relive that terrible night.

"How about from the beginning, and how you met my cousin," Damon said, and when I looked into his pretty eyes I could tell he was upset. For some reason, my wolf wanted to be closer to him, so to calm him and my wolf down, I went over to him and stood in front of him before I placed my hand on his arm.

"Damon, I went on one date with Eric, and that night he raped me."

Chapter Six

Damon's POV:

Punching the wall "I will kill that 5mutherfucker when I get my hands on him," I yelled as my wolf demanded to be set free to hunt down that piece of shit cousin of mine that raped my mate.

"Damon, you need to calm down! Look at your mate, she needs you," Joshua suggest through our pack link. Pausing in my rant of rage, I looked a Rachel and saw that she was standing beside me with her hand on my shoulder, trying to calm me down with tears running down her face. I should have consoled her, and there I was only thinking about my feeling.

"Rachel, I'm sorry my cousin did this to you," I said as I pulled her into my arms and just held her as she cried. Every fiber of my being was on edge, and I was out for blood. As I looked around the room, all the guys had the same expression on their face as I had on mine. We were pissed. Shannon was crying into Lamont's shoulder as he held her while he looked at me.

"Rachel, why didn't you tell us?" Shannon asked wiping her tears with the back of her hand.

"When I came home, I did everything I could to forget that night; I didn't want anyone to know what had happened to me. I just wanted to forget that night, Eric, and the scars he left on my mind and body," Rachel said as she lifted her shirt and showed us the scars on her back and stomach. When I saw the scars on her beautiful body, all I could think about was all the pain I would inflict on Eric when I got my hands on him.

"Rachel, tell us what happened that night, if you can," I said as I sat down in her office chair and pulled her on my lap.

"To make a long story short, I meet Eric in my African-Americans studies class and he seemed like an alright guy. All that semester he had asked me out, but I kept turning him down. It was something about him that didn't seem right," she replied as she wiped the tears from her face. She looked down at me when I grabbed her hand and started to rub her palm. When we were kids and she would get upset, doing that would always calm her down.

"What made you finally go out with him?" Ty asked sitting on the edge of his seat.

"Well on our last day of class, he asked me out again, just to go to the movies and dinner and I thought since we would be in a public place, what could be the harm of two friends hanging out? So, after the movie and dinner we got back to my apartment and after saying good night, I went inside and locked my door," she said when she paused to wipe her tears.

"Rachel, you can stop if you want to, we all will understand," I suggested while rubbing my hand up and down her back as I was battling my wolf, who was demanding to be set free to go hunt Eric down for hurting our mate.

"No, I'm tired of hiding this from everyone. So, later that night I was lying in bed and I heard footsteps, but I thought it was Kasey, my roommate. So, I went back to sleep. The next thing I knew, someone puts a rag over my mouth and just before I passed out, he turned on the lamp on my nightstand and said, "Let's see if this pussy is as good as everyone thinks." Then I guess I blacked out. When I woke up, he was pulling up his pants and I was naked with blood everywhere. When he looked down and saw that I was awake, I quickly jumped up and reached for the lamp. Before he could grab me, I hit him over the head with it. As quickly as I could, I grabbed my robe and I ran out the door. As I was running down the hallway, I could hear him yelling, "I will make you pay." That night, I went to Professor Brown's house, and explained everything to her, except that Eric was my attacker, she helped me clean my wounds and pack my things. Then we waited for my parents to come get me the next day."

"It all makes sense now! When you came home from school, you wouldn't let any of the men in the pack next to you or touch you, except for dad and Lamont. You were so closed off from us and none of us could figure out why," Shannon said as she walked over to us and hugged her sister. As they held each other, they started crying again.

It was killing me inside that I hadn't protected her from my cousin. Instead, I was all over the country looking for my mate, and she had been there the whole time.

"So now that we know everything, what's the game plan?" Andrew asked as he stood up, and then walked over to the window and looked out.

"Well, the way I see it, there's a spy in our pack for Eric to get that close to take those pictures and we need to find out who," Lamont suggested as he also stood up, and Shannon walked back to him and wrapped her arms around his waist.

Sighing, "I think we need to call this alpha meeting a little sooner. I would suggest in the next two days if you agree Rachel. I would also like to have a meeting with our packs and officially announce that we are mates. Hopefully, the spy will make Eric show his hand first out of rage that he can't mate you," I suggested as my stomach turned into knots, just thinking about him trying to mate with Rachel. Then I felt Rachel grab my fist and pried my hand open and kissed my palm. Instantly taking me from anger to lust in two seconds flat.

"Damon, I agree with you," Lamont stated then he looked at Rachel, who was looking at our hands. Then she looked at me, and then at everyone in the room.

Sighing, "If this is the only way we can get rid of this asshole, then let's do it." she stated with so much determination, I felt so proud to have her in my life, and I planned on making sure she knew it.

Chapter Seven

Rachel's POV

"Damon, I need to talk with you alone," I whispered in his ear, as my palms begin to sweat.

"Sure, let's go!" Damon replied looking into my eyes with so much understanding and love, my heart leaped for joy.

Standing up, "Guys, we'll be right back," I stated as I led Damon to the office door.

"Have you guys eaten dinner yet?" Shannon asked just as I opened the door.

"No, we haven't and I'm starving," Ty replied smiling while looking out the window.

"You're always hungry," Andrew joked as he stood up from his seat on the sofa.

"Well then, since I just finished dinner, let's go eat and you two can handle your business and join us in the dining room," Shannon suggested causing me to realize again how much my little sister had grown up. She cleaned up and cooked with the other women of the pack. I guess you could say, she, not the same spoiled little sister, I remembered before going to college.

Looking at Shannon and smiling, "That fine with me." I replied before I looked a Damon, who was smiling at me.

"That's cool Sha," Damon added as he laced his fingers with mine, sending tingles through my body.

"Alright, let's eat," Joshua suggested as we walked out of my office.

As I led Damon up the staircase and they headed to the dining room, I knew that we needed some alone time. It's been years since we've seen each other or even talked.

Walking toward my room, I knew what needed to be done for both of our pack's sake, but after everything that had happened with Eric and I needed to know what Damon was thinking. I was just hoping he didn't let his cousin come between us.

Arriving at my new bedroom door, which I'm was still getting used to since it uses to be my parent's suite, but just before I came home, my parents had it redecorated for me.

As I opened my door, I could feel the tension building between us and it was making me go crazy.

Sighing, "Alright Damon, what do you think about this whole mess?" I asked as I walked over to the bay window, to put some much-needed space between us as he shut the door.

When I didn't get a response, I turned around and he was standing behind me, with an intense look on his face. I almost got scared, but then I remembered he would never hurt me. I hated how he uses to sneak up on me like that. Then it hit me like a ton of brick, "Damon, we need to talk." I said as I backed away from him. My wolf was attracted to his as well, but I couldn't let her take over as he did. Even though we are both Alphas, he had more training, so I had to be careful.

Looking in his eyes, "Damon, please get a hold of yourself," I cried as he grabbed my arm and pulled me up against his body, causing me to start struggling against him.

Then as if someone had cut on a light in his head, he looked at me as if he was seeing a ghost.

"Rachel, I'm so sorry," he said holding me in his arms. Had it been anyone else I would have kicked his ass in the balls, but he's my mate and best friend, so I'd let it slide that one time.

"Damon, it's alright! Believe me, I understand why your wolf took over," I said as I stepped back from him. I felt my wolf starting to go crazy again and needing to be close to him so that we could complete the mating process.

Shaking his head, "Rachel, I feel like an ass, for treating you just like my cousin," he said stepping back from me with such a lost and sad look on his face, making me want to cry.

"Damon, what the hell are you talking about? Yes, your wolf took over, but you couldn't help that. That asshole cousin of yours knew what he was doing and enjoyed it. I know you would never hurt me, which is why your balls are still hanging and not in your throat," I joked, then we smiled at each other.

Chuckling, "You always had a way with words," he joked while tapping the tip of my nose. I hit his hand away as he laughed. When we were younger, Damon's laugh always made my day.

"Alright, Mr. Funny, what do you think of this mess I've gotten myself into?" I asked looking him in his eyes. Damon has the kind of eyes that just don't lie, but to anyone else, they can be downright scary if you get on his bad side.

"Right now, all I care about is your safety. I know that with everything that's happened with my cousin, that you may not be ready to complete the mating process. So, we will take things as they come," Damon replied pulling me back into his arms. Damn that man was too good to be true. I have waited for my mate all my life and there he was the whole time.

Smiling, "Damon, I don't want Eric's actions to dictate how I live my life. I have waited all my life to find my mate, and here you are. I know we have a lot ahead of us, but now I want to focus on just us," I replied as I put my arms around his strong and muscular neck. Damn, he felt so good against my body. His intoxicating smell of the woods and masculinity was making me quiver with need.

"I hate we wasted so much time looking for each other when we could have made each other happy and loving each other," he confessed while looking into my eyes and with one look, I knew he loved me as I've always loved him.

"How about we stop living in the past and start working on the future?" I asked just before I pressed my lips against his.

Chapter Eight

Rachel's POV:

"This feels amazing," I thought as I tighten my arms around Damon's neck and he grabbed two hands full of my butt and lifted me off the floor. His lips were so demanding, yet so gentle as if he was battling with himself. Then he nibbled on my bottom lip asking for entry, which I gladly gave, and the moment his soft and velvety tongue touched mine, it was like firecrackers went off causing us both to moan out in ecstasy.

Before I knew what had happened, we were on the bed and Damon was on top of me ripping off my t-shirt while I was ripping off his black one. As our hands caressed each other's my body, I felt like I was on fire and I needed more. I flipped Damon over and climbed on top of him, and as I sat up, I looked at that gorgeous man and realized he was all mine.

"Rachel, are you alright?" Damon asked as he ran his hands up and down my thighs, making my center quiver with need and desire.

"I'm finally happy and complete now that I have you back in my life," I replied as I laid down on top of him and kissed his lips.

"Baby, I feel the same way and I don't want to waste any more time. I want to cherish you in every way," Damon stated as he flipped us back over while making me laugh.

Smiling, "How about we focus on the cherishing part and less talking Mr. Alpha?" I asked as I ran my hands down his muscular chest, causing him to moan and growl. Looking into his eyes, I saw the love and lust that was mirrored in my own and I needed him so badly.

Pulling his face to mine, I started placing butterfly kisses on his face, while enjoying the feel of his masculine jaws. When I reached his juicy lips and once our lips touched, the sparks flew, and we started ripping each other's clothes off as we explored each other's curves and memorized every inch.

Lying on the bed with our body fused together, we pulled apart to get air while looking into each other's eyes.

"Rachel, tell me now if you want to wait," Damon panted between breaths. Damn, how did I get so lucky to have a mate that cares about my feels above his own?

"I'm sure! Now, stop talking and make love to me," I demanded as I brought his head down and pressed my lips to his causing us both to growl with need.

The moment Damon entered me, I felt so complete and full. He was so caring and gentle, and feeling his warm skin under my hand was so exhilarating. I found myself craving more. The way he kissed my neck as he dug deeper inside me, made my world tilt off its axis. I couldn't form a coherent thought if I tried. I knew that I never want that moment to end. As our moans started to fill the room, and our bodies started to gleam with sweat, I felt the wonderful sensation of my climax building at the bottom of my stomach and I wanted more. As I started to gyrate my hips and meet his thrust, Damon's hold on me tightened and I never wanted to be released. Hearing his moans was almost my undoing, then it was like a bomb went off all around us, because we bite into each other's shoulder at the same time and the room was instantly filled with a beautiful white light. The more intense we became the brighter the light became until we both climaxed with such intensity that our bodies felt as if they had exploded into a million pieces.

Trying to catch our breaths, Damon laid down on the bed beside me and pulls me on his chest.

"You are so amazing, and I'm so glad I waited for you," he whispered as he ran his hand up and down my back- causing shivers of excitement to start again.

Straddling his hips and running my hands up and down his chest, "I'm glad I waited too. Now, can you explain what that light was all about," I asked while smiling down at him.

"I'm not sure what that meant either, but tomorrow we can meet with the elders from both packs and get some answers," he replied as he ran his hands up and down my thighs, causing my center to pulse with need and a moan escaped my lips.

Looking into his lust filled eyes, I knew he was ready for round two just like me. Lying on top of him, I brought my lips to his, and instantly I found myself lying under his sexy and warm body. He started entering me, one slow inch at a time, and then we started picking up the pace. I knew at that moment, that I would never get tired of making love with that amazing man. Thankfully, the bedrooms are soundproof, because, between the moans, growls, and screams, we would have woken the house.

Falling back on the bed and gasping for air, we look at each other and burst out laughing like old times.

"Can you believe all the time we have wasted, when we could have been together and started a family?"

Damon whispered as he pulled me on his chest once again and started caressing my jaw with the back of his hand.

"All that's behind us now! We are together now and if I not mistaken, we just started our own family," I reminded him as I remembered what my mom told me about the mating process with alphas and that the first mating is to start the next line of alphas.

"Are you saying you may be carrying my pup now?" Damon asked as he sat up with his back against the headboard and pulled me to him, so I was straddling his hips.

"Well if what my mom told me is true, when we first mated and marked each other, I was supposed to become pregnant. That might explain that bright light from earlier," I replied as I ran my hand up and down his arms as I looked into his eyes.

"Baby, you have made me the happiest man in the world," He confessed just before kissing me softly on the lips. Which I had no problem reciprocating, as it seemed we were starting round three.

Chapter Nine

Damon's POV:

As I watched Rachel sleep while she laid on my chest, I realized how much she meant to me and how blessed I was to have her as my soul mate. After our amazing night together, I felt more connected to her than ever before. I knew that I may sound like a wuss and all, but you don't understand what it was like to search all over the world for someone, and then you found out that they had been there the whole time.

As I gently swept her soft and curly hair out of her face, as she softly snores in her sleep, I tried to imagine my life before she walked back into it and I couldn't. After our discussion about her being pregnant, I knew she was nervous about being a mom, which I could sense through our bond as mates, and that's why I hadn't confirmed that her assumption was right. Her scent had already changed.

After what she said the night before about what her mom told her about the mating process, Rachel knew she's pregnant, but she was also worried about the situation mess with my cousin.

With her being pregnant, I had to deal with Eric's ass, before he hurt her and our pup. Just thinking about him being near her made me see red.

As if she could sense my mood change, Rachel snuggled closer to my chest as I held her in my arms. I didn't want her stressed out over his punk ass, so I knew I needed to deal with him soon.

"Joshua, are you still here at Rachel's?" I ask opening my mind link.

"Yeah, we're in the dining room eating breakfast," he replied.

"I need you to get our best fighters and have them here in a few minutes," I replied as I eased Rachel off my chest onto the bed.

"Damon, what's going on?" Joshua asked.

"I'll discuss it when I get downstairs and make sure Lamont is there too," I replied just before putting up a block and looking at Rachel as she smiled in her sleep as I started to get dressed.

Moments later, "I hope that smile on your face is for me," Rachel said suddenly causing me to look up from buttoning my jeans.

"Yes, it is," I replied as I sat on the bed and started putting on my tennis shoes as she sat up and wrapped the bed sheet around her. She looked remarkable as she blushed and looked so innocent.

"Where are you going? I thought that we could spend the morning in bed," she suggested just before she dropped the sheet and smiled so seductively. Man, if it wasn't for my asshole cousin I would have taken her up on her offer, but her safety came first.

"How about I go get us some breakfast and we meet back here in ten minutes," I suggested as I kissed her on her neck.

Smiling, "Alright! Since I need to shower, you have ten minutes mister," she joked before pecking me on my lips and running to the bathroom laughing.

Shaking my head and laughing, I headed out of the room shutting the door behind me.

* * * *

Entering the dining room, I find Joshua, the guys, Devin, Kathy and four more of my best fighters sitting with Shannon, Lamont, and three other guys I didn't recognize. As soon as they saw me they all stood up.

"Damon, is my sister alright?" Shannon asked from her spot next to Lamont, who sat at the head of the table. I took my seat at the opposite end with Joshua on one side of me and Andrew on the other side.

"Rachel is fine for now, and I plan on keeping it that way," I replied looking around the table and looking each person in the eye until they lowered their head out of respect.

"I wanted you all here so that we can come up with a plan to take care of my cousin Eric, now that we know he's behind the attacks. Rachel and I have fully mated, and she's carrying our first pup. Since Eric is a threat, he needs to be dealt with now," I demanded slamming my fist down on the table as my anger for Eric escalated as I thought about him hurting my mate.

"What about the Alpha meeting in two weeks? I thought we were moving it up and then we were going after him," Lamont asked.

"That all changed when Rachel became pregnant. I won't let my family get hurt by this asshole," I stated. Just as I was about to speak again, I felt a sharp pain in my head and I screamed as it felt like someone took a sledgehammer to my skull.

"Damon, what the hell?" Ty yelled as everyone crowded around me.

"I don't know, one minute I'm fine the then next my head felt like it was going to split open," I replied just as I thought about Rachel and took off running upstairs. My heart was drumming in my ears as I ran in Rachel's room to find it empty and the window was broken. As I ran around the room calling her name, I know she wasn't there, and my heart was breaking. I can hear everyone yelling and crying, but right then I could only focus on Rachel and getting her back.

"Everyone shut the fuck up and let's go find my baby," I yell before I leaped out the window and shifted in midair.

Chapter Ten

Rachel's POV:

"Damn, I can't believe I waited this long to have sex," I thought as I looked at myself in the mirror and laughed.

Since Damon insisted on getting us some food, I decided to take a much-needed shower. As I looked at myself, I realized that my skin was glowing, and I felt so complete and happy for the first time in my life. Turning on the shower, I couldn't help but think about the previous night and how amazing it was to share myself with the only person I've ever loved.

Thinking about the things we had done the previous night, I couldn't help blushing. Damon made me feel as if I matter to him and that I had finally found that one person that would make me their number one priority. As I showered and ran the luffa sponge over my skin with my eyes close, it reminded me of how Damon placed butterfly kisses all over my body, as his hands caressed and mesmerized my body while taking me to ecstasy.

Then as my hand reached my stomach, I froze. "I'm going to be a mother," I thought as the conversations with Damon came to mind.

It was amazing to think that we created something so special and I knew some people would say it was too soon, but I felt that our baby was created out of the love we had for each other. Our baby would have a happy and memorable life, and even at that moment, I would protect it with my life. The mess with Eric had me on edge because being pregnant changed the situation and I would kill that asshole before he got his hands on my baby.

"Mom and daddy will keep you safe," I whispered as I rubbed my hand over my still flat stomach.

After cutting off the shower and stepping out of it, I wrapped a towel around me before I heard a noise in the bedroom.

Smiling, "Damon, must be back," I thought as I dried my hair. I started thinking about being in his strong arms again, as the need to be close to him became unbearable. I pulled on my robe and then opened the bathroom door. When I walked into the room, I found it empty.

Walking further into the bedroom, "Damon!" I said, just before I felt a sharp pain on the back of my head. Just as the room started to spin, I looked around at my attacker and I froze.

Looking into their hate-filled eyes, "Why would you do this to me?" I asked just before darkness consumed me.

Chapter Eleven

Damon's POV:

"Where in the hell is she?" I yelled as I paced back and forth in Rachel's office. After searching for hours, we lost Rachel's scent and I'm was going crazy. I've tried reaching her through our mate bond, but she wasn't responding.

"Damon, we have both packs best trackers looking for her and we will find her," Joshua said as he looked out the window.

"How in the hell did her scent just disappear?" Lamont asked as he sat on the couch holding Shannon as she cried.

Sighing, "I don't know, but I have to find her," I stated as I sat down in Rachel's office chair and put my head on her desk as I tried to get my thoughts together.

Just thinking about her with my crazy ass cousin was driving me crazy. I had heard of the crazy things he had done in the past to women. Eric was the type of person that liked to play mind games and torture his pry. To him, it was all a game and it was just my luck he had his eyes on my mate.

After a few minutes, Devin and Kathy walked into the office.

"What did you find out about Eric?" I asked as I sat back in the chair and looked at them.

Looking around the room, "We found out where he is keeping her, but we have a problem," Devin stated before looking into my eyes then down at the floor. Just so you know, I trusted Devin and Kathy with my life, and they were just like family. For both of them to be nervous to tell me what they found out, it must have been bad.

Leaning forward in my seat, "Devin, just spit it out," I yelled getting very impatient with everyone.

Clearing her throat, "Eric doesn't just have Rachel, he has her parents and yours," Kathy replied.

Hearing their news caused me to see red and taste for blood. I didn't know if I could contain my wolf anymore.

"What the fuck!" I yelled as I sent everything on the desk flying onto the floor.

"That mutherfucker is dead!" I scream as I pounded my fist on the desk.

"Damon, calm down! We need to come up with a plan to get them back." Andrew suggested putting a hand on my shoulder.

My thoughts were all over the place. How did he get our parents? I just spoke to them two days before and they were having a ball in California.

"Something isn't right! This has to do with something other than Rachel, for him to take our parents too," I said out loud as I walked over to the bay window and looked out.

"Where are they keeping them?" Lamont asked.

"In a warehouse, two cities over from here. From what we could see, it's heavily guarded by his pack of rogues," Devin stated.

"Joshua and Lamont, I want you two to get both packs here in an hour," I said sitting back down and looking at both betas.

"Alright," they both agreed and left the office followed by Shannon, Devin, and Kathy.

"Damon, we will get them back," Ty said from his seat on the sofa.

Shaking my head, all I could think about was Rachel and our baby. I prayed to the Moon Goddess that they were alright. To add more to the equation, I must worry about our parents and getting everyone home safe.

As the rest of the guys were discussing a plan of attack, I'm wondered what Eric really wanted.

Chapter Twelve

Rachel's POV:

"Damn, my head hurts like hell!" I thought as I woke up and my head started pounding. When I tried to move my arms, I realized I was tied up to a chair. Looking around the room, it looked like an abandoned building and the only furniture in the room was the chair I was sitting in and a table that looked old and dirty.

As I looked around, I saw one door and there weren't any windows. As I tried to free my hands, the door opened and in walked a big muscular guy with an ugly scar on the right side of his face and he was carrying a tray.

"Who the hell are you and why am I tied to this damn chair?" I yelled and before I knew what was happening he had slapped me across the face. Then he yanked my head back, so I was looking into his face.

"Shut the fuck up and you won't get hurt. No, I take that back, either way, you're going to get hurt, but don't rush it," he said jerking my hair back again before letting me go and setting the tray on the table.

"So, you're the piece of ass Eric is going through all this trouble for?" He asked eyeing my body with lust in his eyes.

"I don't know what the hell you're talking about. I just want to go home," I said as I started to wonder where Damon was and if he was alright.

"This is your home now," he sneered before he walked out the door and slammed it behind him.

"Like hell, it is," I yelled as I tried to free my hands, but it was no use trying because the ropes didn't give even after using my alpha strength.

As I tried to regroup, my thoughts turned back to Damon and if he was alright.

"Damon, please be alright," I thought as I pictured him in my mind and tried to feel him through our bond.

"Rachel!" I heard him call out, but I thought I was hearing things.

"Damon!" I replied as I prayed it was him.

"Rachel, please answer me!" he yelled

"Damon, where are you?" I thought. Thank the Moon Goddess, for a minute I thought I was going crazy.

"Are you alright? I've been going crazy," he replied.

"I'm fine! They have me tied up in a room," I replied.

"We know where you are and we're coming to get you," he replied.

Just hearing his voice in my head, I felt safer.

"Please hurry," I replied just as the door opened again, and it was my worst nightmare, Eric who walked in looking evil as ever.

"It's good to have you home baby. You've been a bad girl since we've been apart," Eric said as he shut the door and walked over to me smiling.

"Damon, Eric is here please hurry," I said before blocking Damon, so I could focus on Eric.

"In fact, I hear you've been a very bad girl with my cousin," Eric stated as he walked behind me. Then he yanked my head back by my hair. What the fuck was up with those assholes and yanking my hair.

"Eric, why did you bring me here?" I asked hoping to buy Damon some time.

"That what I like about you Rachel, your straight to the point," he said as he ran his hand down the side of my face while making my skin crawl from his touch. Don't get me wrong, Eric wasn't bad looking, but once you get to know him, his manipulations and evilness will turn you off.

"I can't tell you much now, but I can tell you that once everyone gets here, we all can see the grand finale together. Then we can start our life together. That is after we kill that pup you're carrying," Eric said looking at my stomach with such hatred, that I scooted back in my seat. That fool was crazy if he thought I was going to let him kill my baby.

"Eric, what are you talking about?" I asked, wondering who else was coming.

"Rachel, Rachel, Rachel! How dumb do you think I am? I have had someone watching you all this time. I know about everything between you and my cousin, and I can still smell him on you," he yelled as he smacked me across the face. I pissed him off more by not showing pain, so he smacked me again. This time, I tasted blood inside my mouth, but I still wasn't giving that asshole the satisfaction of knowing he had hurt me.

"So, you want to be a tough girl? Baby, before all this is over, I will make you scream," he said yanking my head back, and then he kissed me. That guy really was crazy, and it was no telling what he would do, so I had to buy Damon some more time.

"Eric, what is this all about? You could have any girl you want, so why me?" I asked looking into his eyes.

"Why you, you ask? Well, you see, this all started long before you came into the picture. This was between me and my dear cousin, but then you entered the picture making it more interesting," he replied.

Shaking my head, I began to wonder, what could have happened between him and Damon? From what I remember Damon saying, he wasn't allowed to have anything to do with Eric, because their fathers didn't get along.

"What could Damon have done to you?" I asked getting more confused by the minute.

"See, it's not what Damon did. It what our parents and your parents did, and now we must finish it," he said smiling before he walked out the door and slammed it behind him.

"What the fuck was he talking about?" I wondered.

Chapter Thirteen

Damon's POV:

"Thank the Moon Goddess that she's alright," I said as we all sat in the office waiting for the two packs to gather.

"What did she say?" Lamont asked as he sat on the sofa.

"Nothing much, other than they had her tied up in some room, and that Eric was coming into the room, then the connection was broken," I stated as worry started to creep into my mind and I started to wonder if Eric had done something to her to break the connection.

"Did she say if she was hurt or anything, or if she had seen your parents?" Ty asked from his seat beside Lamont.

"No, she didn't! Plus, I'm not sure she even knows they're there," I said as I looked at the map on Rachel's desk of the warehouse, where they are keeping them. Thank the Moon Goddess that Devin and his connections were able to get us the blueprints of the building.

"Alright, it's time to head to the meeting," Andrew stated as he stood up.

As I stand up, I realize that not only did I have to lead my pack, but also Rachel's, even though Lamont was their beta. I'm Rachel's mate and the only Alpha there. Thank the Moon Goddess that we all grew up together, so they know and trust me. Walking out of the office with everyone following me, I thought about Rachel and how strong and independent she was. Then how I must represent both of us and stand strong in front of our people so that we could get her and our parents back.

Opening the front door of the packhouse, I was greeted by a yard full of people who I had come to call my family and friends. Seeing me, they all became silent and waited for me to speak.

"I have called you all here because a lot has happened in the past twenty-four hours, and I needed to bring everyone up to speed. I know most of you and I hope to get to know the rest of you that I don't. My name is Damon and I'm the Alpha of the Jade Pack. This is my beta Joshua and my close friends and pack mates Ty, Andrew, David, and Ben. You already know your beta, Lamont. First, I want you to know that Rachel and I are mates and that we have fully mated," I stated looking everyone in the eye as they started cheering. I wished Rachel was there to see how happy they are. As I waited for them to settle down, I thought about our packs and how they will react to the rest of my news.

"Alright there's more, this morning Rachel was taken by my cousin Eric and we also found out that he has our parents. I know this is a lot to take in, but we don't have much time and I need both packs to understand the situation and I need fighters to volunteer to help us get them back. I know I'm asking a lot of you, but this is your Alpha too and I wanted everyone to know what was going on." I said as I looked around the crowd.

"Now, there's one more thing that needs to be dealt with. We have a spy in our camp that has worked with my cousin so that he could take Rachel. This person has taken pictures of Rachel in her room sleeping and during other private moments to give them to my crazy cousin. This spy is also the one that took Rachel to my cousin this morning," I said as my anger started to rise and it had taken every fiber of my being not to rip them to shreds, as they stood there like they hadn't done anything.

"Greg, why don't you tell us why you betrayed your pack," I said as I started to walk up to him as everyone gasped and started looking at him with such hatred. Greg was Rachel and Shannon's first cousin and we all were best friends growing up. Greg and Rachel were just as close as she and I were. Rachel trusted Greg with her life and for him to betray her like that was unforgivable.

"Damon, what are you talking about?" Greg asked while looking around as Lamont and the guys surrounded him.

"At first, we couldn't figure out who was always around Rachel and could get that close to her to take those pictures. Then we got to thinking, who had the equipment to take that good of quality pictures and at first, when you came to mind we dismissed it because we knew you would never hurt Rachel. Then when we went into the room where Rachel was taken from, and we found your scent all over the room. Plus, laying on the floor was one of your earrings that Rachel had given you for your birthday after you two went together and got your ears pierced. Which is funny, since its missing from your ear now," I said as I grabbed him and lifted his ass off the ground by his neck.

"I'm going to say this one time, and if you value your damn life, you will tell us what we want to know. What does Eric plan to do with Rachel and my parents?" I asked as I tightened my hold on his throat making him gag.

Gasping, "All I know is that he plans to kill them in front of you to make you suffer," Greg replied before I let him go and he fell to the ground, but Ty and Andrew picked him up and held him. I felt like someone had punched me in the gut. Rachel and our parents are being held just to hurt me, and for what? I don't even know, because I had only met Eric twice and we were kids then. So, why does he hate me so much? It didn't make any sense.

"Alright, everyone that wants to go with us, we are leaving in an hour. Joshua and Lamont have everyone ready. Ty, you and Andrew take Greg to the basement and tie him up. I want someone to watch him at all times until this is over, then Rachel can deal with him when she gets back," I said looking at Greg one last time before they started to carry him off.

Leaving everyone outside, I walked back into the office, to find Shannon sitting on the sofa crying.

"Sha, everything will be alright," I said as I sat beside her on the sofa and hugged her as her tears overtook her again.

"Damon, promise you will bring them home, they're all the family I have," she said between her tears.

"Shannon, I promise that I will bring them home," I replied as I wiped the tears from her face and looked her in the eyes.

"Thank you, "she said as she hugged me, then stood up and walked out of the room, leaving me alone with my thoughts.

I prayed that I was able to keep that promise, but I needed to figure out what Eric was up too first. I guessed the only way to find out was from the source. I just hoped he's ready for the fight of his life.

Chapter Fourteen

Rachel's POV:

"Why in the hell did I go out with his crazy ass," I thought after Eric walked out of the room.

I mean, in college I had guys asking me out all the time, and the one time I decided to go with someone, it had to be his crazy ass and he also happened to be Damon's cousin. As I looked around the room for any way to escape, I found a window, but it's boarded up. That's why I didn't notice it before. Having that ray of hope for freedom, I needed to get my hands freed. As I played with the ropes, dumb ass from earlier walked back into the room.

"I see you're still in one piece, Eric must really like you," he joked as he ran his hand through my hair causing me to jerk my head away from him. I instantly felt sick just from being touched by him.

"Don't touch me asshole!" I shouted at him and he only laughed at me before he smacked me across the face and pulled my head back by my hair.

"I'll do what I want when I want to bitch," he shouted before roughly kissing me. When he pulled away, I had his spit all over my lips. It took everything in me not to throw up.

"You'll learn your place before this is over," he said chuckling as he backed away from me and picked up the tray from the table. Hearing him say that renewed my determination to get free and get back to my mate and pack.

"What is your name?" I asked needing to get as much information as possible.

"My name is Riley, but don't worry, we will become best friends when Eric is through with you," he replied before laughing and leaving the room.

The instant that door closed, I tried to get Damon through our connection, and just when I was about to give up I felt him.

"Damon!"

"Rachel is that you?" he asked, and I finally released the breath I had held.

"Yes, baby it's me, please tell me you're on your way," I begged as I continued to work on the ropes.

"We will be leaving in a few minutes, are you alright?" He asked, and I could feel the anger and fear that he was trying to hide from me.

"I'm fine; I just want to get out of here. Eric is acting really weird," I said just as I felt the ropes loosen, thank The Moon Goddess.

"What do you mean he's acting weird," he asked as a wave a fear hit me through the bond.

"Damon, he has some vendetta against our parents and us, but when I tried to get it out of him, he just clamped up and said I will see soon," I replied as the ropes continued to loosen and I pulled my hands free.

"Rachel, I know he has something against me, but don't worry, we will be there soon," he said as I untied my feet.

"Alright! I was able to get untied from the chair and I'm going to try to escape," I replied as I stood up, but I became dizzy and had to sit back down. What the fuck was wrong with me?

"Rachel, please be careful and just hide until we get there," he requested as I stood up again and walked quietly to the door and listened.

"I will be careful, and I love you," I said still listening for anyone in the hallway.

"I love you too," he replied before I ended the connection.

After not hearing anyone in the hallway I walked back to the boarded-up window and slowly tried to pull the board away from it. As I put all my strength into it, the board slowly came off, but just as I got the board off, it made a loud noise when it broke into two pieces. A few seconds later, I heard someone running down the hall, and I knew I had to hurry. So, I jumped out the window and thank The Moon Goddess for my wolf reflexes, because I was able to land on the ground without breaking any bones.

Instantly, I started running and I knew they were right behind me, so I shifted into wolf form and ran as fast as I could.

At first, I was lost and not sure which way to go, then as I came to a wooded area, I realized it was the woods we all use to play in as kids, so I kept running toward home. The closer I got home, the more paws I heard hitting the ground behind me. Using all the energy I had left, I started running faster and faster, and just when I thought I would pass out, I saw the open field where we held our meetings and parties. Just when I started to reach out to Damon through our bond, something jumped on my back and knocked me to the ground.

When I twisted around and knocked them from me, I stood up on my paws and got in a defensive stance and growled as the grey wolf, who also had stood up and growled at me. Suddenly, eight more wolves came up behind the grey wolf, and they also started growling at me. As fear consumed me, I started to back up as they advanced toward me. Then I heard a loud growl come from behind me. Fear paralyzed me as I felt as if I was surrounded and had nowhere to go. Seconds later, I smelt a familiar scent, and when I saw a black wolf come and stand in front of me with a ton of other wolves circling around me and growling at the other wolves, I knew I was safe, and I collapsed on the ground just before everything went black.

Chapter Fifteen

Damon's POV:

"Is everything set to go? Rachel is trying to escape on her own, so we need to leave now," I stated to Joshua and Lamont when they found me sitting in Rachel's office. After talking to Rachel, and knew she was going to take the risk of trying to escape by herself, which had me scared to death.

"Yes, everyone is ready and waiting for us outside," Joshua replied as I stood up and walked around the desk.

"Alright, let's go then," I stated as I walked out the office headed outside. As I walked outside, I thought about Rachel and our pup and getting them home safe. I also thought about our parents, and I hated not telling Rachel about them being taken too, but I couldn't add that stress on her.

Arriving outside, I found most of our packs standing there ready to go.

"Alright everyone, I want to thank you for fighting with us to get Rachel and our parents back. I know that you are taking a big risk coming with me and I just want you to know how grateful I am for your help," I said as I looked at each person in their eyes.

"Lamont and Joshua already told you the plan, so let's go," I added just before I shifted into my wolf form and took off running with everyone following me.

As I ran, I tried to connect with Rachel, but she didn't respond. Just when I was about to give up, I felt a rush of fear hit me and I instantly knew it was her, so I pushed myself harder to get her. Just as we got to the edge of our property, I heard something running straight for us.

"Everyone stand guard! Someone is heading straight at us," I yelled through our mind link as I slowed down. Then a scent hit me, and my wolf went crazy. Running faster, we come across a white wolf growling at a group of rogue wolves, and I instantly knew the white wolf was Rachel.

When she looked at me, she collapsed to the ground and changed back to her human form. As I went to her, our packs surrounded us. Changing back to my human form, I checked her to make sure she wasn't injured and other than a few scratches, she was fine. Changing back into wolf form, I looked at the rogues that wanted to hurt her, and my anger turned into rage. All I saw was red as I charged at the grey wolf that was in front.

Grabbing his throat, I quickly snapped his neck and threw him to the ground. When I looked around, our pack had taken care of the rest of them. Taking one last look around, I quickly went back to Rachel. Seeing her on the ground and not moving, caused my heart to ache and I knew I needed to get her back to the packhouse.

"Lamont and Joshua, change back and put Rachel on my back. Also, call the doctor and have him meet us at the house," I said through the pack link as I laid down beside Rachel. Quickly they did as they were told, and after making sure she was secure on my back, I took off running as fast as I could.

As I ran, I prayed that Rachel and our pup were alright. I could hear her breathing, so I knew she was alive. When we reached the house, Shannon and the pack doctor were standing outside. As they lifted Rachel off my back, I quickly changed back into my human form and pick her up and carried her into the house, followed by the doctor.

Arriving in her room, I softly laid her on the bed and after kissing her lips, I stepped back so the doctor could check her out. It was killing me that I had to leave her, but I knew that she had to be seen by the doctor.

"Damon, is she alright?" Shannon asked me when I stepped into the hallway shutting the bedroom door behind me.

"She has a few scratches and bruises, the doctor is taking care of her now," I replied as I leaned against the wall and closed my eyes. My head started to feel like someone was taking a hammer and hitting it.

"Damon, are you alright?" Ty asked as he and the guys walked down the hall toward us.

"I'm fine, just worried about Rachel and our pup. Plus, I'm trying to figure out what to do about our parents," I replied as I ran my hands over my face and stood up.

"Damon, now just focus on Rachel, then we will get your parents back," Andrew suggested as he put a hand on my shoulder.

"He's right! We're here for you two and we will get them back," Lamont stated as he put his arm around Shannon and they smiled at me.

I knew they are trying to comfort me, but all I could think about was what Eric would do to our parents when he realized Rachel had escaped. Just as my thoughts started thinking about Eric sadistic methods of torture, the doctor walked out of the room.

"Is she alright, Dr. Jones?" I asked as I walked up to him.

"Rachel is resting now! She's dehydrated and has minor scrapes and bruises. She'll be alright after a few days of rest and drinking plenty of fluids," he replied.

"Is the baby alright?" I asked.

"The baby is fine also, but Rachel needs to rest for both their sakes. I will be back later to check on them," he replied before walking down the hall.

After the doctor left, I walked into the bedroom and found Rachel sleeping peacefully and looking like an angel. Sitting on the bed beside her, I softly lifted her hand to my lips and kissed it. As I looked at her, I thought about all the shit she has been through, and I vowed that I would make it up to her.

After a few minutes, I felt a hand on my shoulder and when I looked up, I found all our friends standing there.

"Damon, why don't you get some rest while she sleeps, then we can plan how to get your parents back," Lamont recommended as everyone else nodded in agreement.

"Alright, for just a few minutes," I agreed as they smiled, and then started to walk out the room shutting the door behind them.

As soon as they were gone, I laid down beside Rachel and pulled her into my arms. As we laid there, I started thinking about our future and how I was going to spend the rest of my life making her happy. Then I realized as sleep started to claim me that the only way we could be happy was for me to deal with Eric once and for all.

Chapter Sixteen

Rachel's POV:

The faster I ran the closer they became. As I ran through the woods, I suddenly ran into a stone wall and they had me cornered. As I turned around to face my enemy, I knew I was outnumbered, but I wasn't going down without a fight. Suddenly, I felt someone clawing at my side, and I released a glass breaking scream.

"Rachel baby, Rachel," is all I hear, and when I opened my eyes, I saw the last person I expected to see, Damon.

"Damon," was all I could get out before he had me in his arms, holding me close to his chest as he sat back against the headboard.

"Baby it's ok, your home and safe," he said as he rubbed my back and kissed my forehead.

"Damon, how did I get here?" I asked because the last thing I remembered was being in the woods.

"We found you in the woods, about to be attacked by a group of rogues, but we quickly dealt with them. Then I brought you back here, so the doctor could check you out," he replied as I sat on his lap and leaned back so I could see his handsome face.

"Damon, thank you so much. I remember jumping out the window and running as fast as I could. Then everything started looking familiar to me when one of them jumped on my back and I shook him off. Then I remember seeing a black wolf before everything went black," I said as I put my arms around his neck.

"That wolf was me and I'm glad we got there when we did," he said as he hugged me.

As we held each other, I thanked the Moon Goddess that I was back in his arms and I felt whole again.

"Rachel, there something you should know," Damon stated and by his tone, I knew it wasn't good, so I sat back and looked into his eyes.

"What is it?" I replied as I braced myself for whatever it was.

"Rachel, Eric didn't just take you. He took our parents also," he said as my whole body froze.

"Damon, please tell me you're joking," I yelled before I jumped up and ran to my dresser and pulled out a pair of blue jeans and a white t-shirt. I started getting dressed, while Damon sat on the edge of the bed.

"Baby, you need to rest. If not for yourself then think about our pup," he said making me stop instantly just as I finished getting dressed.

All that time I had been worried about escaping, and not once had I thought about our baby.

"Oh, Moon Goddess! Did I hurt the pup when I jumped out the window or when I shifted to run home?" I asked as my tears flooded my vision and I put my hands on my stomach.

"No baby, you and our pup are fine, but you need to rest for both your sakes," Damon replied as he pulled me into his arms and held me as I cried. I felt like I had a ton of bricks on my shoulders, but just being in his arms, I felt as if I was finally safe and that I had someone to share the load with.

Looking up at Damon, I saw that he had tears in his eyes and I knew he was hurting just as much as I was.

"Damon, we need to call a meeting and form a plan to get our parents back and deal with Eric once and for all," I said as I dried his tears with my thumbs and he did the same to me.

"Baby, I don't want you to go with us when we attack Eric," Damon stated as he looked at me.

"Damon, there is no way in hell am I going to sit back while he has our parents," I shouted as I stepped back from him as my temper started to rise.

"Rachel, I know that you want to be there when we rescue our parents, but baby you need to rest. The doctor said you need to rest for a few days and I don't want anything to happen to you or our pup," Damon replied and I knew he was just worried about us.

"Damon, I understand what you're saying, and I will be careful with you by my side, but there is no way I will sit by and let you face that asshole alone," I stated with my hands on my hips, while looking him straight in the eyes.

"Rachel, I know when to pick my battles with you, but your safety is not something I take likely, so if you come with us, you will not leave my side. Are we clear?" He asked standing toe to toe with me. Now, I knew I was pushing it and Damon would hog tie me to my bed unless I agreed to his terms.

"Alright, I will be careful, and I won't leave your side," I agreed, but we both knew that once the fighting began, it would be hard to keep up with each other without getting ourselves killed.

"Now that this is settled, let's go raid the kitchen, then we meet with our packs and form a plan," I said as I put my arms around his waist and he hugged me.

"Sounds like a plan," he replied as he kissed me, and then he led me to the door.

As we walked to the kitchen, I thought about our parents and feared what Eric was doing to them. As if he could sense my thoughts, Damon pulled me into his arms as we continued walking to the kitchen.

Chapter Seventeen

Damon's POV:

"What am I going to do with this stubborn woman? Doesn't she realize I'm just thinking about her and our pup's safety? But no, she is determined to come with us when we attack Eric," I thought to myself as we sat at the dining room table with everyone else eating the breakfast that Shannon had made for everyone.

"Rachel, you can't go with them to attack Eric," Shannon stated as she sat down beside Lamont with her own plate.

"Why not, I am the Alpha of this pack, plus he has our parents," Rachel stated putting her fork down and looking at her sister. I could feel Rachel's anger starting to rise. So, I grabbed her hand and smiled at her.

"Rachel, you are pregnant now, and you need to be thinking about the pup and what's best for him or her," Shannon stated as tears came to her eyes. Lamont put an arm around her and dried her tears with his napkin.

"Shannon, I can take care of myself. Plus, Damon will always be by my side," Rachel replied as she picked her fork up and started eating again. Looking over at Shannon, I could tell she didn't believe her sister any more than I did when we made that agreement upstairs.

"Rachel, I've already lost my parents and I don't want to lose you too," Shannon replied as her tears overtook her, causing Rachel to get up and walk over to sister, before pulling her into her arms.

"Shannon, you're not going to lose me, and we will get our parents back, I promise," Rachel stated as she wiped the tears from her sister's face as they smiled at each other.

As I watched the sisters, I realized how much pain my cousin had really caused them, and I vowed that he would pay for every tear that they had shed because of him. I also prayed that he hadn't taken his anger about Rachel's escape out on our parents or worst killed them to teach us a lesson. As the thought entered my mind, I felt Rachel in my thoughts.

"Damon, we can't think that way. We must believe that they're alright. If they aren't, Eric will pay with his life," she said through our mate link as she took her seat again and grabbed my hand.

"You're right! We need to think positive until we have proof that proves otherwise," I replied back through the link as I smiled at her, and she returned it with that sexy smile of hers.

"Alright! So, what plans have we come up with, so we can get our parents back?" Rachel asked before putting a fork full of eggs in her mouth. Damn, just watching her chew was sexy as hell and it was making my jeans become very tight. As if she had read my mind, she winked at me, making me blush. Could you believe she had me blushing, I was so whipped?

"Before you two came downstairs, we were talking, and we think its best if we go in tonight, so we will have the darkness to cover us. Plus, with you knowing a little bit about their hideout, that gives up an advantage over them," Joshua stated as he put his fork on his empty plate.

"Plus, we have the blueprints of the warehouse. So, we have that also as an advantage," Lamont added as he finished eating also.

"Damon, if it's alright with you, I suggest we get both packs together and follow their plan," Rachel said as she looked at me.

"I like the plan, so let's get both packs here by six, so we can get ready and leave," I stated as I looked at Rachel then at everyone else at the table.

"Before we go, there still have one problem to take care of," Ty said looking at me and I instantly knew what he was talking about.

"What problem?" Rachel asked looking at me confused.

"Rachel, we found out who was helping Eric in your pack. Plus, he was the one that took you to Eric," I stated as I grabbed her hand, as she looked around the table, then back at me.

"Who was it?" Rachel asked looking up at me. I hated to be the one to tell her because he was a part of her family.

"Rachel, it was our cousin Greg," Shannon stated beating me to it.

"What the fuck? How could he do this to me and to his own family," Rachel yelled as she jumped up from her seat and started pacing back and forth.

"Rachel, we have him in the basement with around the clock security watching him," I said as I stood up and pulled her into my arms and hugged her as she let her tears flow.

I wish I could have taken the burdens off her shoulders. First, Eric took her, then she escaped to find out he had also taken our parents. Then she found out that her own cousin had betrayed her and was helping Eric the whole time. I knew Rachel was strong, but there's only so much a person can take.

"Rachel, let's deal with Greg after we get back. Right now, everyone needs to rest up for tonight and meet outside the packhouse at six o' clock, so we can get ready and leave," I said looking at my friends and Lamont.

"You're right, I'm feeling very tired suddenly," Rachel replied just before I picked her up in my arms as she wrapped her arms around my neck.

"Alright guys, get everything set up and we will see you at six," I stated before I walked out the room heading upstairs. When I looked down at Rachel, I found her sound asleep.

As I carried her up the stairs, I prayed that Rachel and our pup survived the battle ahead of them. If I had anything to do with it, they would, because I won't be leaving her side for one minute. Walking into our bedroom, I gently laid her on the bed and quickly undressed her, before putting her in the nightgown she had on earlier. Then I undressed down to my black cotton briefs and crawled into the bed beside her. After getting comfortable, I pulled her into my arms and just decided to enjoy this moment with her as sleep took over. Just as I felt my eyelids getting heavy, I wondered what Eric's big secret was about our past.

Chapter Eighteen

Rachel's POV:

As I'm getting dressed, my stomach was in knots and I could feel Damon watching my every move as he also was getting dressed in jeans and a t-shirt like me.

"Damon, stop worrying. I feel your emotions loud and clear," I said as I walked over to him and sat in his lap before he wrapped those sexy and muscular arms around me.

"Baby I'm sorry, but I just don't like the element of surprise he has over us. Plus, you still need more rest," he replied before kissing my neck. Feeling his soft lips and warm breath on my neck was making my wolf go crazy and my hormones are running on overdrive.

"Damon, everything will be fine. Plus, we will deal with everything together. So, let's go and get it over with," I stated as I stood up and grabbed his hand.

"Alright my warrior princess, just promise me that you will be careful," he stated pulling me to him as he stood up.

"I promise," I replied as I kissed his chin and started walking toward the door with him following me.

As we walked downstairs, I could hear our packs assembling outside and at that moment I felt great pride to be their leader and to have such a strong mate to lead by my side. Opening the door and walking outside hand in hand, Damon and I faced them with our heads held high.

"Alright, everyone knows the plan and I want to thank everyone here for standing with us at our time of need. After this craziness is over, we will get better acquainted, since we will be one unit now that we have mated, but all that will be discussed later at the celebration. So, let's go take care of these assholes who threaten our homes and family, then come back here and celebrate a new beginning," I said as I raised our hands and our people cheered. Looking over at Damon, he was watching me with a proud smile glowing on his face. It should have been a sin to look that good.

"Alright, everyone get into your groups and remember that these are rogues we are up against and one scratch or bite is deadly. We are going to hit them from all four corners and surround them. We are getting assistance from area alphas that are watching Eric and his pack for any new developments or movements. Go let's go hard and strong, and everyone watches each other's backs," Damon stated before he turned to me and kissed me softly on the lips. Then he led me off the porch and in front of the pack were Joshua and Lamont and the rest of the gang were standing.

"Alright guys, let's do this," I stated just before transforming into my wolf form. Then looking around me, I saw that everyone else had followed my lead and transformed. Looking to my left stood my beautiful mate and to my right stood my beta and on Damon's left was his beta with the rest of the guys behind us.

"Let's go," Damon yelled into our heads as he took off with us right behind him.

As we ran, I prayed for everyone's safety and that it would be the end of the madness with Eric, so that we could be one big happy family. Also, so our pup could have a happy and peaceful life.

* * * *

After what seemed like hours, we met up with the other packs and we followed them to where Eric was keeping our parents. Yes, I had been there, but I hadn't seen much with being locked in that room and jumping out of that window to escape. Looking at the warehouse, it looked like a fortress and we were lucky to have the blueprints to it, so we could know where the rooms are and how the building flowed. It also helped to know if it had a basement, which it didn't thank the Moon Goddess.

"There hasn't been any movement in the last few hours and my informant tells me that your parents are being kept in the center room. They are being heavily guarded, and Eric is with them now as we speak," Alpha Kinley of the Shadow Pack stated after we all transformed. Alpha Kinley was a dear old friend of our fathers.

"Alright, if we stick to our plan, then we can deal with this quickly and get everyone out safely," Damon replied looking at me and I nodded in agreement.

"Let's go then," Alpha Kinley replied and we all stood up and transformed.

Taking one last look at me, Damon took off and I ran off behind him.

Chapter Nineteen

Damon's POV:

After taking one last look at Rachel, I released a mighty howl to signal everyone to attack and I took off toward the building where they were keeping our parents. Soon as we all entered the compound, we ran head first into Eric's pack and the fighting began. As I fought with a grey wolf, I looked around for Rachel and saw her fighting two brown wolves. Needing to get her, I quickly snapped my opponent's neck and just as I was about to help Rachel, I saw Eric standing in the doorway of the warehouse watching us with a big smile on his face.

"That asshole is mine," I yelled as I looked over at Rachel to see her looking at me with her opponents laying on the ground.

"Rachel, there's Eric, let's end this," I said to her while looking back at Eric, who just stood there smiling at us with his rogues around him like that was going to save his ass.

"Baby, let's go," Rachel yelled as she took off running toward Eric.

As we ran toward them, Eric and his rogues backed into the warehouse. Taking one last look behind me, I saw that our packs were right behind us, leaving Alpha Kingly and his pack to finish the rest of Eric's pack.

Once we got to the door, I slowed down to look around for any traps. Not seeing anything, I lead the way into the warehouse, to see our parents tied to chairs in the middle of the room with bruises on their faces. "These mutherfucker are dead," I thought to myself as my temper started to rise.

Walking further into the room, my pack quickly handled the guards, leaving Eric to me and Rachel.

"So, I see you finally made it," Eric stated with that stupid smile still on his face. It took everything in me not to rip out his throat, but we needed answers first.

"Eric, you have two minutes to tell us what this is all about, before I kill you," I yelled after I transformed back to my human form.

"All in due time, how are you doing Rachel, my love," Eric said eyeing Rachel from head to toe. That fucker was crazy to be eyeing my mate in front of me.

"First of all, I'm not your love, and secondly I'm doing great because you will be dead soon," Rachel replied with her hands on her sexy hips. Just watching her made a smile formed on my face, but I quickly covered it up.

"Rachel, I'm so disappointed in you, I thought you had better taste than to mate with my low life cousin here," Eric replied as he nodded his head in my direction. Not able to take it anymore, I grabbed him by the throat and banged him against one of the steel beams in the room.

"You better tell me why you did all this, or I will snap your neck," I yelled as I tighten my grip, then I felt a soft hand on my shoulder. I looked back to see Rachel, which calmed me down a little, but not enough to release him.

"Eric, just tell us what is going on," Rachel asked as she walked over to our parents and started to untie them, along with the help from pack members.

"Rachel, he is crazy," Kelly, Rachel's mom cried as she hugged Rachel.

"I know mom, but you're safe now," Rachel replied as her dad, Thomas hugged them both.

"Do either of you know what big secret Eric is talking about?" Rachel asked just as Tammy and John, my parents were released, and they walked over to me since I was still holding Eric.

"I think I know what this is all about," my mom stated as she looked between me and Eric and caused everyone to pause and look at her.

"Mom, what's going on?" I asked as I released Eric and hugged her as tears started to fall down her bruised cheek. My guards quickly grabbed Eric, so he wouldn't run.

"Damon, I know that we should have told you sooner, but I didn't know how," she cried making me hold her tighter as my dad rubbed her back. I looked over at Rachel to see her in her parent's arms as they looked at us.

"Mom, whatever it is, we can work through this," I said as I dried her tears. I hated to see my mom upset or crying.

"Damon, we should have told you a long time ago, but we didn't know how. When you were born, you had a twin and he was kidnapped two days after you were born," My dad stated causing me to I feel like someone had kicked me in my stomach because I knew where this was headed.

"What happened after the kidnapping?" I asked as I sat down on one of the chairs that our parents just vacated.

"Our packs followed them to a compound on the outskirts of the state line and when we got there we attacked them," Thomas replied, I had almost forgotten they were here.

"So, you all followed the kidnappers and then what?" Rachel asked as she walked over to me and put a hand on my shoulder.

"Well, when we got there, we found out that my brother was behind everything and somehow he escaped our attack," My dad replied as he sat beside me.

"Whatever happened to the baby," Rachel asked.

"He was left to fend for himself, with an asshole who beat him every day," Eric stated causing everyone to look in his direction.

This couldn't be happening, there was no way that Eric crazy ass could be my brother.

"Eric, we didn't know who you were until you locked us up and started dropping hints. Then when I looked into your eyes, I knew you were my baby," My mom said as she walked up to Eric and touched his cheek.

"Damon, we're sorry we didn't tell you this sooner, but I always hoped he would find his way home to us," she said as she walked over to me and placed a hand on my shoulder.

"Alright, so he's my long-lost brother, but that doesn't make up for the hell he put my mate through," I yelled as I stood up looking Eric in the eye.

Chapter Twenty

Rachel's POV:

"I must be going crazy," I thought to myself as I listened to Damon's parents, as they told him about his long-lost twin brother and that he was in fact, Eric.

What really pissed me off was that Eric was trying to act all sad and mistreated, when in fact he happened to be the person that made my life a living hell. Standing here watching it all unfold, I could feel the anger, confusion, and pain that Damon was feeling through our bond. I wanted to hold him and let him know everything was going to be alright, but at that moment he was standing toe to toe with Eric, and I needed to help him stay in control.

"Damon, look at me," I said as I stood beside him and grabbed his hand.

When he looked at me, I could see that he was fighting his wolf for control.

"Baby, everything is alright. Eric won't hurt me again," I said as I looked into his eyes, then I kissed him, which he quickly responded to.

After feeling him take back full control, I stepped back and faced Eric.

"What did you mean about him not hurting you again?" My father asked as he walked over to us.

"I guess I may as well tell my secret since everyone is telling theirs. While I was in college, Eric kept asking me to go out with him and I kept turning him down. Then the last night at school before you came and picked me up, I decided to go out with him. So, to make a long story short, Eric ended up raping me and has been spying on me, using my cousin Greg to help him. Then he kidnapped me and brought me here, but I managed to escape. Damon found me before his rogues could catch me and bring me back," I replied as Damon wrapped me in his arms, as I watched our parents' shocked faces, then my dad's face filled with anger as he held my crying mother.

"Eric, how could you do something so hateful to Rachel?" Damon's mom asked him as tears filled her eyes.

"I knew she was only playing hard to get, so I just did what we both wanted?" Eric replied with a smile on his face.

Before anyone could react, I had my hand around his throat and had slammed him into a steel beam as I cut off his air supply.

"Rachel, he's not worth it! He should spend the rest of his life in jail. Killing him is letting him off too easy," Damon said as he stood beside me and put his hand on my shoulder. His touch started to calm me down, as my grip on Eric's throat lessened. Then out the corner of my eye, I saw Eric pull out a silver object and before I could react, he plunged it into Damon's chest. Without thinking, I ripped out Eric's throat and threw his body against the wall. Within seconds, I was on the ground holding my mate, who was losing a lot of blood.

Looking down at him, "Damon, please hold on! Baby, you can't leave us! Our pup and I need you," I yelled through my tears, as I held pressure on the wound after I pulled the silver knife out. His wound would start to heal quickly on its own with him being an alpha, but then I saw that the tip of the knife had broken off in his wound, which would keep it from closing.

"Rachel, I love you and our pup," Damon whispered as he dried my tears with the back of his hand.

Kneeling down beside me, "Damon, you are going to be fine son, the pack doctor is waiting at Rachel's packhouse. So, we need to get going, but you need to fight," his father told him, and then he kissed Damon's forehead before he stepped back so that Damon's mom could see Damon, as his own tears started to fall.

As each of our parents talked to Damon, I prayed to the goddess to let my mate live so we could grow old together and raise our family, as my own tears continued to fall. After all the parents were standing there looking at Damon, he became very weak and his skin became very pale, and I knew we needed to get going quick.

"We need to get moving, he doesn't have much time and we need to get him to the doctor. I need four people to carry Damon to one of those jeeps outside," and before I could finish speaking, Damon's best friends were already standing beside us and started to carefully lift Damon off the ground. I followed them out of the building.

"Damon, please hold on baby. I'm are right here," I pleaded as they gently laid him on the back seat with his head in my lap.

"Rachel, I love you so much," Damon whispered looking into my eyes.

"I love you too," I replied through my tears. I felt as if my heart was being ripped out because I could feel his pain and I was also dealing with my own.

"Rachel, I'll drive you two back," Joshua stated as he and Lamont jumped into the front seats, and quickly drove off leaving a cloud of dust behind us.

"Damon, you have to keep your eyes open baby," I yelled when he closed his eyes and my heart started to beat as if it was going to jump out of my chest.

When he opened his eyes, something about them was different, almost as if his soul wasn't in his body anymore.

"Joshua, drive faster. He needs to change into his wolf form so that his wound will heal, but we need the doctor to get the silver piece that broke off the knife out of the wound first," I yelled through my tears as Damon became even paler.

Chapter Twenty-One

Rachel's POV:

"I'm going out my fucking mind! Damon, please wake up, we need you," I cried as I sat at his bedside.

It had been two months since that fateful day, and Damon's body had healed, but for some reason, he wouldn't wake up, and I was at my wit's end about what to do. In the two months, my stomach had doubled in size due to us expecting triplets, and I wished that Damon had been there with me for our first sonogram, but the six godfathers stepped in and went with me along with both sets of our parents.

So, there I was sitting there looking at my sleeping mate, as the guys come in the room.

"Hey mommy, how's the patient doing today?" Joshua asked.

Smiling down at Damon, "He's finally getting his color back, and hopefully he will wake up some," I replied as I ran my hand down his jaw.

"He will just give him some time. You know the doctor said that the poison that Eric had on that knife should have killed Damon, but he is still fighting, so don't give up on him yet," Lamont stated as he placed his hand on my shoulder.

Sighing, "I know I need to be patient, but I feel like I'm going to lose it," I replied as my tears consumed me.

"Rachel, we are here for you and our godkids until Damon is on his feet again," Ty stated as the guys pulled me into a bear hug which made us all laugh.

"Hey, I close my eyes for a few minutes, and you guys already making moves on my woman," a voice said out of nowhere making everyone freeze.

"Please tell me you guys heard that too," I replied as we all looked at Damon, but his eyes were still closed.

"Yes, we heard it too," Joshua stated as we all circled the bed.

"Damon, say something else please," I cried as I grabbed his hand.

But instead of speaking, Damon squeezed my hand and a smile formed on his lips.

"I'm going to skin him alive if he doesn't stop playing with me," I thought to myself.

"No, you won't," Damon said out loud for everyone to hear, as he finally opened his beautiful eyes.

"Damon, when you are fully healed, I'm going to beat your butt," I said as I sat on the bed beside him.

"I look forward to it," Damon replied smiling.

Seeing him smile was the best present anyone could have given me on my birthday, which was that day.

"We're going to leave you two alone, so we can let your parents know that he's awake. Also, before we forget, Happy Birthday Rachel," Lamont stated as the guys pulled me into another bear hug which made everyone laugh again.

Sitting back on the bed, we watched as the guys left the room and shut the door behind them.

"Damon, I was so scared that I was going to lose you," I cried as I laid down beside him and put my head on his chest.

"Rachel, I will never leave you and our pup," Damon replied as he rubbed my enlarged stomach.

"Yeah about that, we are expecting more than one baby," I said as I sat up and looked into his eyes.

"Alright, that's cool! So, how many are we having?" He asked smiling.

"Three, and because we both are alphas, our offspring will grow faster than a regular wolf pregnancy. So, we have two more months to go before they arrive," I replied just as our room door busted opened and Lamont and Joshua ran in the room.

"What is going on?" Damon asked as we sat up on the bed.

"Guys, we have some bad news," Lamont stated looking at us with tears in his eyes.

"What is it?" I yelled as fear started to race through my veins.

"Somehow Greg got free and escaped taking Shannon with him," Joshua stated

"You have to be kidding me," I yelled as I jumped up and ran out the room heading downstairs. Just as I reached the living room, I saw my parents holding each other as my mom cried. At that moment it felt like someone had put a ton of bricks on my shoulders, and my knees buckled under the weight. Just as I came close to the floor, a pair of strong arms grabbed me.

"I got you, baby," Damon said as he picked me up and everything turned black.

Chapter Twenty-Two

Damon's POV:

The last thing I remembered before everything went black, was the excruciating pain in my chest and the room deeming around my mate's beautiful face as she started to cry. I felt her anger and pain soar through my body and I knew I had to fight and hang on because I couldn't leave Rachel and our pup after just getting them in my life.

Then the next thing I knew, I hear her crying and our friends trying to console her. I could also feel her sadness and pain and I needed her next to me. When I finally had her back in my arms I felt complete, plus I found out we were expecting three pups. Then, as usual, all hell broke loose again, with Rachel's cousin, Greg causing the trouble instead of my crazy brother, Eric.

After my mate fainted from all the stress and being pregnant, I placed Rachel softly and safely on the couch. Then I turned and faced our betas, "Alright, someone get me updated on this mess."

"Damon, after Eric stabbed you, Rachel killed him. Then we had to rush you back here, so the doctor could get the piece of silver that broke off the knife out of your wound, so you could shift. Now two months later, Greg has escaped and took Shannon with him," Joshua replied as he looked down at Rachel then back to me.

"Has anyone started tracking him, and how in the hell did he get free and grab Shannon?" I asked as I started to pace the floor, as our mothers held each other and cried, while our dads stood ready for battle.

Just seeing those two like that, made me fear for anyone that crossed their paths.

"Damon, we found Devin on the basement floor unconscious with a big gash in his forehead, but he alright now. When we followed Greg's scent, it leads us to another abandoned warehouse about two hundred miles from here," Joshua replied from where he stood to look out the window.

"He must have grabbed Shannon when she was outside playing with the kids," Ty stated.

"Damon, Shannon isn't due to deliver for another couple of months, but she was having some complications and was put on bedrest. Plus, we were getting married tomorrow," Lamont stated as he wiped his tears.

"Damon, please bring my baby back," Kelly pleaded from her place in my mom's arms.

"I will do everything in my power to get her back today," I replied as I looked at my mate sleeping so

Peacefully, and I hoped I can get her sister back before she woke up and cut my balls off for leaving her here.

"Alright, let's go get Shannon back, and everyone please be careful. Greg may have rogues working with him," I said just before I took one last look at my mate, and then proceeded to walk out the front door.

"Lamont, when we get there, I want you to focus on getting Shannon out of there, and the rest of us will focus on Greg and his help if he has any," I stated as we stood outside in front of the house.

Looking before me, I found a large group of our combined pack, and they were ready for war.

"Everyone knows why we are here, and now it's time to fight. I thank everyone for volunteering and on my command let's go," I stated as I looked each of them in their eyes.

Seeing we were all in agreement, I turned and ran toward the forest.

Chapter Twenty-Three

Damon's POV:

Anger and frustration ran through my veins as we ran through the woods after Greg and Shannon. All I could think about was Shannon being hurt or going into labor early from the stress.

As we approached the warehouse, I could smell the stench of the rogues, but I could also smell something that smelled familiar, but I can't place it. Reaching the warehouse, we all transformed and staked out the building.

"Damon, where did he get all these rogues on such short notice? We killed all the ones that were with Eric?" Joshua asked standing in front of me.

I was thinking the same thing, with Greg just getting free that morning.

"Do you think they had two compounds?" My dad asked as he stood beside Joshua.

"It looks that way, and does anyone recognize that smell in the air?" I asked as it started to nag me the more I tried to figure it out.

When I looked at my dad, he looked angry as hell, and my instincts were telling me to get prepared for some craziness.

"What's going on dad?" I asked as I put my hand on his shoulder.

"Thomas, don't you recognize that scent?" my dad asked, causing me to look at Rachel's dad as he sniffed the air, and a shocked expression came to his face.

"It can't be!" Thomas yelled looking over at my dad.

"Will someone please tell me what's going on?" I yelled as I became frustrated with all their secrets.

"How about I tell you what's going on?" Someone said as they walked up in front of us.

When I looked up, I came face to face with someone, who could have been my dad's carbon copy.

"What the fuck is going on?" I yelled as I looked over at my dad then back at the stranger.

"Son, this is your uncle Ronald. The man who raped mother even though we were fully mated, who was behind Rachel getting hurt, and who is also your biological father," my dad replied as sadness filled his eyes.

Confusion and anger consumed me because I was tired of the lies. "Was everything about my life a lie?" I thought to myself.

"Damon, I'm your real father," Ronald said as he stepped closer to them with his group of rogues behind him growling.

The closer that man came toward us, the tenser I became. I had heard the horrific things he had done, and that was the reason my parents had cut off communication with him.

"If he's my father, how did I become Alpha of your pack?" I asked the man who had raised and loved me.

"Son, your mom was the true Alpha of our pack, but after everything happened, she wanted me to step up and take over. Since you were our only child, you became the alpha. Even if Eric hadn't been taken, you would have still been alpha, since you were the eldest by twenty minutes," my dad replied.

"Damon, I've waited years to approach you and tell you the truth and to offer you my kingdom, but I need to get rid of your mate, so I could have your full attention," Ronald said causing everyone to look at him.

When I looked at him, all I felt was rage, and I don't know if it was because he had raped my mom, or because he was behind all the pain Rachel had gone through, but in the blink of an eye, I had transformed and charged toward Ronald.

Chapter Twenty-Four

Rachel's POV:

Feeling as if a weight was sitting on my chest as I tried to sit up, and the bright sunlight coming through the window blinding me, I started to panic as I looked around the room and wondered why I was back in my bedroom.

"Rachel honey, here let me help you up," my mom cried.

Looking to my left, I saw my mom's tears stained face, and on my right, I saw Tammy, Damon's mom. Instantly, I started to wonder where the hell Damon was. Swinging my legs off the side of the bed, both of our mothers stood in front of me with tears in their eyes, and as I placed my hand on my huge stomach, the events of that morning came rushing back to me causing my breath to hitch. Tears began to roll down my face as I began to think about the safety of my sister and her pup.

"Baby, everything will be alright," my mom whispered as she sat down beside me and put her arm around my shoulders.

Sitting on my other side, "Your mom is right! You know that Damon and the guys will not rest until Shannon and her pup is home safe and sound," Tammy added as she dried my tears with her hand.

Tammy Jackson was like my second mom since I spent so much time at her house as Damon and I were growing up.

Jumping up as fear raced through me almost paralyzing me, "Where is Damon?" I asked as I placed my hand back onto my stomach as it felt as if my pups were doing cartwheels.

Watching our mothers as they shared a look before looking over at me, I instantly knew their answer before they opened their mouth and rage flooded through my veins. I could feel my breathing become labored, and my body started to shake as my hands balled up into a tight fist.

"Rachel, you need to calm down. It's not good for you or my grandbabies to add more stress to yourself," my mom said as I started to pace back and forth.

"How could he just leave and not tell me?" I yelled as I threw my hands up in the air.

"Sweetie, Damon loves you, and he knows how much you love sister. After making sure you and the babies were alright, he quickly rushed after Greg. He's focused on getting her back before she goes into early labor," Tammy replied as she stood in front of me, causing me to look into her eyes.

"Tammy is right honey! Damon is doing what he should be doing as one of the Alphas of this pack and looking out for his family. You need to focus on taking care of you and my grandbabies," my mom added as she pulled me into her arms and hugged me.

I knew that they both were right, but I was worried about my mate and sister's safety. Taking a deep breath, I felt my fear squeezing my heart, as tears rolled down my cheek.

Taking another deep breath and wiping my tears from my cheek with my hand, "You both are right, but if he has one scratch on his body, his butt is mine," I joked as I hugged them both.

"I agree," Tammy added smiling.

"Me too! Now let's go get you something to eat, and before you know it, they will be back," my mom suggested as she led me toward the door.

"Sure, it's not like I have much of a choice," I joked causing them both to smile. I wasn't hungry, but I knew that I needed to eat for my pups' sake. Plus, I needed to keep my strength up to take care of my pack.

Just as I almost reached the bottom of the stairs, I felt a rush of confusion and anger flow through our mate bond, causing me to grab the banister, as my other hand went to my chest.

"Honey, are you alright?" my mom asked, who was standing at the bottom of the stairs looking up at me with a frown on her face.

Taking a deep breath, and then walking down the rest of the stairs as tears flooded my eyes, "No I'm not! Something is wrong with Damon," I yelled as I rushed to the front door. Just as I pulled it open, the room started to spin, and I felt as if someone was clawing my chest. Stumbling onto the front porch as I gasp for air, I saw a group of young kids playing in the yard, as my vision started to dim. Still determined to reach my mate as my heart rate started to accelerate, I could tell my body was starting to shut down and I started to fall to the ground. I heard my mother scream just as I fell into a pair of strong arms and darkness consumed me.

Chapter Twenty-Five:

Damon's POV:

With all my strength, I went after Ronald and tried to rip out his throat, but he dodged my attack. That fool got it twisted if he thought he was going to get away with first hurting my mom, and then hurting my mate. As we started to circle each other, I could see that everyone else had shifted and was fighting the rogues that had accompanied Ronald. Turning my attention back to Ronald, just as he swung his front left paw at my face, which I quickly dodged. Looking him in his eyes, I waited for him to charge at me. Seconds after that thought passed my mind, he leaped at me and I met him midair as I went for his throat again.

That time I did grab some of his meat, just not as much as I had planned. He also managed to rake his claws across my chest as we continued to battle. The pain I was feeling was excruciating, but even that wasn't going to stop me from killing that bastard that had caused me and my family so much pain. Stepping back to get my barring, I saw a rogue trying to sneak up on me from my left, but all too quickly Joshua intervened and tackled him to the ground.

Turning my attention back to Roland, I noticed that he was breathing heavy and staggering a little from the blood loss and I knew I needed to strike quickly. Getting in a defensive stance, I watched his movements and I could tell from the way he was watching my every move that he was also deciding when to strike me. As I waited patiently, I looked for any sign he was going to attack, and when he leaped in the air to jump on me I met him midair again, but this time I was able to catch his neck fully in my mouth and I bit down with all my strength crushing his windpipe. He was able to claw my shoulder, but nothing was going to get me to turn him loose.

When I felt his body go limp and slump to the ground, I snapped his neck to make sure he was dead, before releasing his neck from my grip. Looking down at his lifeless body laying before me, I didn't feel any remorse for killing the man that was also my biological father. All I felt was hatred for him, and I hoped he rotted in hell for all the pain he caused.

Looking around me, I saw that most of the rogues were either dead or running back into the woods. Everything in me wanted to chase them down, but at that moment we needed to find Shannon. Looking to my right, Joshua came and stood beside me and on my left stood Andrew.

"We need to find Shannon," I commanded throughout pack link.

"We've already taken care of that. Lamont and some pack members rushed the warehouse and found her," Andrew replied as we all transformed and pulled on shorts that Kathy had thrown at us.

"They are on their way out now," Joshua replied just before I saw Lamont walking toward me holding Shannon and seeing her bruised and beaten caused my heart to ache.

"Damon, calm down! You are scaring her," My dad demanded as he came and stood next to Joshua.

I took a deep breath as I watched Thomas, who was Rachel and Shannon's father walk up to her and Lamont with tears in his eyes. I took everything in me not to hunt down the rest of those rogues. Then I remembered the one person that was the reason Shannon was even there.

"Where is Greg's punk ass?" I snared as I looked around the field.

"I killed his ass!" Lamont snared causing Shannon to whimper. His whole demeanor changed when he looked down at his hurt mate in his arms.

I could understand him being angry, and I don't blame him for killing Greg. I would've killed the bastard if I could've gotten to his ass. He was their cousin and had betrayed Rachel and Shannon.

"Lamont let's get her home! The pack doctor is waiting for her arrival," Thomas suggested before he kissed his daughter's forehead.

With a nod of his head, Lamont, Thomas and Rachel's pack left heading back home, while my pack and I stayed behind to clean up the mess of dead bodies everywhere. As my pack started a fire and started throwing the dead bodies on the fire, I watched as Andrew and Joshua lifted Ronald's lifeless body and tossed him in the fire, my dad came and stood beside me.

"Son, I understand if you hate me, but please don't turn away from your mother. You are her life," My dad suggested.

"Dad, yes I'm mad as hell about all the secrets you two have kept from me, but that wouldn't stop me from loving either of you. You two loved me and was always there for me no matter what. You not being my biological father doesn't change anything, because you will always be my dad," I confessed before I looked over at him.

"Son, when things happened so long ago, we were trying to keep you from being hurt and being pulled into Ronald's plan to get back at us. I just hate both of our sons had to be hurt in the process and Eric growing up with so much hatred in his heart," My dad stated causing my whole body to tense up.

"Dad, I don't want to think about Eric or Ronald. They both could have chosen a different path, but instead chose to hurt our family and I will never forgive either of them for it," I replied as I watched the last of the bodies be disposed of and my pack started to walk toward me.

"Son, I can understand that, and just know that if you even want more answers or just need to talk, I'm always going to be here," My dad said as he turned toward me and looked me in my eye.

Turning toward him, "I know that dad, and I still love you," I replied as I hugged my dad.

Pulling apart and looking at Joshua when he finally reached us, "Is everything done?" I asked.

Nodding his head, "Yes, it is, and we are ready to head back when you are," he replied.

"Let's go! I know my mate is ready to put my head on a platter right about now," I joked as I thought about Rachel and when she woke up and realized I wasn't there.

"Yeah, you better have a good apology ready when you get back," My dad joked as we started to walk back to the packhouse.

Smiling, "An apology isn't going to fix this," I replied just before I transformed and took off to see my angry mate. I just hope she leaves me in one piece.

Chapter Twenty-Six

Rachel's POV:

"I'm going to kill him!" I shouted as I paced back and forth in my office as I rubbed my belly.

There I was carrying our pups and Damon was out there, risking his life. I could never repay him for going to rescue my sister, but the fear that something could have happened to him was almost paralyzing. As I continued to pace, I heard a loud commotion in the foyer, and when I rushed out my office, the sight before me almost brought me to my knees.

Lamont was holding my sister that I almost didn't recognize because her face was so swollen and bruised. Tears poured down my face as I walked toward him, and the closer I got the shallower my breathing got. I felt like someone was cutting off my air supply. Why would anyone do something like that to someone as sweet as Shannon? She was the sweetest person you could ever know, and there she was hurt and scared.

As my mother and I stood in front of Lamont, I looked into his eyes, "Please tell me that bastard is dead for this?" I snared as my heart rate started to race and my hatred for my cousin reached a new level.

"He died a slow and painful death," Lamont replied before looking down at Shannon as she whimpered in his arms.

"Let's get her upstairs and into some clean clothes as the pack doctor takes a look at her," My mom suggested before she kissed my sister on her forehead.

Taking one last look at my sister, I kissed her cheek before I nodded for Lamont to take her upstairs, with my mom following him.

It was as if I was frozen in place as I thought of what she had gone through, and I almost couldn't breathe again.

"Baby, she is safe now," My dad whispered in my ear as he held me in his arms. I finally let my guard drop and I fell into his arms and cried for my sister and my pain that had been caused by that whole situation with Eric and Greg.

I couldn't for the life of me figure out why my cousin would help Eric in his crazy plan to hurt us. We always treated him like a brother instead of our cousin. After both of his parents were killed when he was five years old, my parents took him in and raised him as one of their own.

Shaking my head, I pulled away from my dad and looked into his eyes, "Where is Damon?" I asked.

"He will be here soon, they stayed behind to take care of the dead bodies," he replied causing me to release the breath I had held.

"Were any of our people hurt?" I asked as I walked back into my office to my office chair and sat down.

Shaking his head, "Just minor injuries, as for the other side, we killed most of them and the rest ran off into the woods," My dad stated as he sat down in the chair in front of my desk.

Nodding my head, all I could think about was my mate and if he was ok when my office door opened, and Damon walked in. Instantly, I jumped up and ran to him. When he pulled me into his arms, I felt as if I was safe and complete again.

"I missed you so much," I cried as I buried my face in his chest, enjoying his masculine scent.

Kissing my forehead, "I missed you too baby," he whispered as he tightened his arms around me.

I enjoyed being that close to him and hearing his heartbeat, and our pups must have too, because they started doing cartwheels in my tummy, and he must have felt their movement, because he stepped back and looked down at my stomach, bringing a smile to my lips.

"Yes, that's your overactive pups. They must be happy too that you are home," I joked before I stood on my toes and kissed his juicy lips.

"I'm going to let you two have some privacy," My dad said before he walked out of my office closing the door behind him.

Then looking into each other's eyes, we kissed. The moment we kissed, it was as if fireworks went off and I couldn't get enough of his taste. I felt like a starving woman as I closed the distance between us and our kiss deepened. I loved the feel of his velvet tongue against mine, and the power and strength he put into the kiss almost sent me over the edge. I couldn't help the moan that came from me as he grabbed both hands full of my butt and pulled me closer to him so that I could feel his excitement.

"Damn, I'm sorry," we heard, and when we looked toward the door, we both growled causing both of our betas and friends jump back.

Shaking my head, "Its fine! Come in," I replied before I kissed Damon's chin and smiled up at him.

"What do we owe for this interruption," Damon joked as he laced his fingers with mine and led me over to my office chair, where he sat down and pulled me onto his lap.

"We came to tell you that all the injured have been taken care of and Shannon is resting now," Lamont replied as he and Joshua sat down in front of my desk.

"Thank you, guys, for bringing my sister back," I said as a tear rolled down my cheek, as I thought about my little sister and what she must have gone through.

"You don't have to thank us, we are family. That what we do for each other," Joshua replied as he smiled at me.

Nodding my head, I looked down at Damon, and he looked so tired, "Damon, what happened out there?" I asked causing him to look up at me and I instantly knew that something else had happened while they were recusing my sister.

"How about we let you two talk about that in private, plus a brother is starving," Andrew joked as he and the rest of the guys stood up and walked toward the office door. Seeing them make a quick getaway, made me even more nervous.

Soon as the door closed, I looked down at Damon and found him looking out the window with a lost look on his face, and it almost broke my heart.

"Babe, what happened," I asked as I turned his face, making him look into my eyes.

Sighing, "I killed my biological father," he replied and instantly my eyes widened, and I couldn't believe what I was hearing.

"Why would you kill John?" I asked still in disbelief.

Shaking his head, "Not John, I'm talking about my biological father and the one behind this whole mess," he replied as he looked back over to the window.

"Damon, I'm confused! I thought John was your father," I said as I turned his face toward me again.

"Not only did I find out I had a twin brother that was a lunatic, but I also found out that my biological father was the same man who I always thought was my uncle. The same man who has had it out for our parents for years, and who helped Eric hurt you," He confessed as he signaled me to stand up.

Standing up, I watched him stand up also and walk over to the window with a lost look on his face, and I couldn't imagine the things that were going through his mind. Everything he thought about his life was a lie.

Walking up to him and putting my arms around his waist, "How did you find all this out?" I asked as I laid my head on his chest.

Sighing as he wrapped his arms around my shoulders, "When we reached the warehouse, he came out and introduced himself. Then the bastard had the nerve to tell me that he had to get rid of you so that I could take over his kingdom, and at the point, I lost it. We started fighting and I killed him," he confessed, and I just hugged him.

"Baby, I'm so sorry," I whispered as I looked up at him.

"There isn't anything to be sorry about. I have two loving parents that love me and have always been there for me, and that will never change. Now, we need to think about our own family and making sure they are loved and protected," he replied just before he kissed my forehead.

"You're right. Now, that the craziness is over, it's time to get ready for our own bundles of joy to arrive in two months," I stated before kissing his chin and smiling up at him.

"I love you so much," He confessed as he looked in my eyes.

The look of love and admiration in his eyes told me more than his words ever could. When he looked at me, I felt so special and cherished.

"I love you too baby," I replied before kissing him again.

As we stood there holding each other, I realized how much my life had changed in just a few months, and I wouldn't change any of it. Yes, there was a lot of secrets that came back to bite us in the ass, but we all came out of it in one piece. We came out of it as a family, and that was something no one could take from us.

Epilogue

Rachel's POV:

"They are too cute!" My mom said as we sat on the front porch watching the kids play.

Chuckling, "You can say that, because they aren't keeping you up at night," Shannon replied causing me to laugh.

As my mother and sister went back and forth, I thought about how my life had changed so much as I watched my two years old son, Adam and my two daughters, Angel and Angela play with their cousin, Devon. The triplets were born a week after Devon. I guess they came early since they were running out of the room or got tired of sharing the same womb. It was funny that even at that moment, they couldn't be separated for a moment without crying for the others, and somehow, they had included Devon into the mix. Which lead to us to making the nursery big enough for all four. I shook my head as I thought about the funny things those pups did and will do in the future.

Since everything had happened with Eric, Greg, and Ronald, our packs were combined, and Damon and I remained the Alphas over both packs. We built a big packhouse in the middle of the two territories, and that was where the alphas, betas, omegas, warriors along with their families resided. In my old packhouse, the elders and married couples resided there and in Damon's old packhouse the younger unmated members resided there.

"Well, I will say they are just as cute as you two were at that age," my mom stated causing me to look over at her just in time to see her wipe her tear.

"Adam reminds me so much of Damon when he was that age. He was always watching over everyone and making sure they were laughing and having a good time, just like Adam is doing now with his sisters and cousin," Tammy added as she also wiped her cheek.

As we watched the kids, sure enough, Angel had fallen and was starting to cry, but Adam helped her up and kissed her cheek, causing Angle to smile. "He was definitely going to be a charmer, just like his dad," I stated smiling at how cute the scene before.

"I hope that's a good thing," Damon joked as he and the guys walked up on the porch, and he came over to me and kissed my lips.

Smiling, "That's definitely a good thing," I replied before I kissed him again and he sat down beside me on the loveseat.

"What are you women up to?" Lamont asked after he kissed Shannon and sat beside her on the porch steps.

"We are talking about how cute the kids are and how much Adam reminded us of his father," my mom replied as we watched my dad and Damon's dad play with the kids.

"May the Goddess help us if he is anything like his father," Joshua joked causing Damon to throw a pillow at him and making everyone laugh.

"I beg your pardon, but my baby was a perfect child," Tammy replied smiling.

"Thank you, mom," Damon added before he kissed her cheek.

Seeing them together, I could only hope that Adam and I will have a relationship that closes.

"I think those four will be more of a handful than all of us were at that age," Damon joked as we watched the kids tackle their grandpas to the ground and started trying to tickle them.

"I think you may be right! Moon Goddess help us," Lamont added causing us all to laugh.

As we watched the kids and the guys joined the tickle fest, I realized how far we all had come. Shannon finally stated to trust being around other men in the packs and was enjoying her life as a wife and mother. My parents and Damon's parents were enjoying being grandparents and getting to spoil them rotten. As for me and Damon, we were a stronger unit than before and each day that passed, our bond became stronger and nothing would ever change that or hurt our family again

By Leanora Moore

Alpha Of My Dreams

A Werewolf Love Story

Chapter One

Jaden's POV:

Let me start by telling you a little bit about myself. I'm
Jaden Griffin and I'm what most people would call your
average teenager if you would call being a werewolf as
being average. I'm eighteen years old, standing at five feet
eight inches tall, with Hersey chocolate skin, and black
naturally curly hair that flows to the middle of my back. I
know some of you may have thought, just because I'm a
werewolf that I should have a perfect body, but if you ask

me, I have an alright body. I've been told that I have the coke bottle figure, with a little extra in the butt and breast area, and I'm cool with that. Did I mention that my dad, James Griffin was the Alpha of our pack, the Redstone Pack, and my mom Ava Griffin was the Alpha Female. I also have two big-headed brothers named Travis, who's my twin and Keith, who just turned 18 and is soon to be the next Alpha when my dad steps down.

"Jaden get your butt down here this minute, or you will be late for school," yelled my mom.

"Ok, mom," I shouted back.

Normally, I would be dragging, because I'm just not a morning person, but today is special. My brother, Travis and I are starting our senior year. Plus, I can't wait to see the new pack that has moved in the next town. They will be going to our school since its considered neutral territory. From what I've heard, they have some fine guys with buff odies. Now, don't get me wrong, I'm still a virgin and I to stay that way until I meet my mate, but there's wrong with looking.

ing a quick shower and dressing in my black h my purple halter top, then adding my s with my silver hoop earring and silver bangles to finish my look. Looking at my watch, I realized I had two minutes before my mom comes into my room and has a hissy fit, and it was too early for that. So, after adding a little purple eyeshadow to my eyes and clear lip gloss to my lips, I rushed downstairs to see my family in the dining room eating breakfast.

"Good morning, everybody," I greeted as I sat down, and my mom placed a plate in front of me with bacon, eggs, and toast on it before she took her seat.

"Good morning baby," my dad replied while reading his paper and my mom just smiled. As usual, my brothers were feeding their faces too much to speak, so they just nodded their heads and kept eating.

Just as I was about to take the first bite of my eggs, we heard a car horn.

"There goes my breakfast," I grumbled as I grabbed my bacon. It had to be my best friend, Keisha Avery coming to pick up my brother and me for school. Keisha and I have been friends since kindergarten and her dad, Eric Avery is our pack's Beta. Grabbing our stuff, we ran out the front door to see Keisha bobbing her head to her music.

"Hi girl," I greeted after opening the passenger door and getting into the car.

"Hi Jaden and Travis, you'll ready to start our senior year?" Keisha asked as she reversed out of our driveway.

"You know I'm ready to graduate, so I can go to college in New York," I replied smiling as I looked out my window. I started wondering if I'll find my mate before I head off to college. I've been dreaming about him since I was a little girl. I've been told that your mate is your other half and the one person that will love you no matter what. Now don't get me wrong, I have dated, but they never lasted long after the guy found out he wasn't getting any of my sweetness.

"You mean so we can go to New York," Keisha replied smiling. Keisha and I both had applied to Columbia University and got accepted.

"I better call New York and warn them about you two," Travis joked from the back seat before putting on his headphones and started listening to his music on his iPhone.

"Hahaha, very funny," Keisha said as she turned into the school parking lot.

After we parked, my brother jumped out of the car and headed toward his friends, which were basketball jocks just like him, which were surrounded by fake Want-A-Be cheerleaders. Now don't get me wrong, they do win cheerleading competitions, but their attitudes are what I don't like.

"Are you ready to see the new meat?" Keisha asked as we followed my brother out of the car.

"Keisha, come on now! You know they are probably nothing, but dogs just like the ones already here," I said as we walked to the front of the school. I know I sounded bitter, but after my last boyfriend, Jason Patterson cheated on me with Samantha Richards, who happened to be the head cheerleader of the want-a-bees'. So, I decided to wait until I met my mate, and avoid all the drama and games.

"You need to quit, you want to see what the Blue Moon Pack looks like just like all the other girls. Plus, I hear their Alpha, Alex Jenkins is fine," Keisha said as we walked inside the front doors of Gold Leaf High School.

As we walked down the crowded hallway to our lockers as Keisha kept talking, I waved at friends from last year and pack members, when I smelt the most exquisite smell that was a mix of the woods and manliness. As I got to my locker, I found the source of the hypnotizing smell, standing across from my locker talking to his friends with his back to me and when he turned around and faced me, I froze and dropped all my books.

Chapter Two:

Alex's POV:

Waking up to my alarm going off, I quickly turned it off and dragged myself into my bathroom to take a quick shower to wake up. While showering, I thought about all that had happened that last year. It had been a hard year for my pack, with my dad, Alvin Jenkins the previous alpha being killed by my Uncle Jerry and his rogue pack during a surprise attack, all because he was always jealous my dad. Since then, I've become the Alpha of the Blue Moon Pack, and we had to relocate, because during the attack they burned down our homes, plus my mom, Jennifer Jenkins needed a fresh start. Watching my mom each day as she tried to act normal, I knew she missed my dad. Plus, losing your mate usually sends you into a deep depression, because it's like you've lost half of yourself, but lately, she had kept herself busy decorating our new packhouse.

After getting dressed in a pair of black Dickie cargo shorts and a white t-shirt and pairing that with my black and white Jordan's, I head downstairs to the dining room where I found my mom passing out plates of sausage, eggs, and grits to my pack members.

"Good morning mom," I said as I kissed her on her cheek as she passed me my plate.

"Baby, are ready to start your new school?" my mom asked me as she sat down to eat her food and as I started to eat.

"Yes, mama! Plus, we're invited by the Alpha of the Redstone Packs for a bonfire at his home tonight. So, we can get to know each other, since they are one of our alliances," I replied before I finished digging into my food.

"I know! I met Ava, the alpha female yesterday while I was downtown picking out some curtains for my room," my mom said as she took my empty plate to the sink.

"Thanks, mom! Alright, everyone, we need to get to school," I said as all my friends finished eating and grabbed their bags.

After grabbing my bag, I walked out of the house toward my new black Dodge Charger trimmed in silver with new chrome twenty-five-inch rims.

"Hey Alex, ready to see if this school got some fine chicks?" my best friend and my beta Jacob Davis asked as he got into the passenger seat. As you may have guessed, Jacob was a stone-cold player, but he was also looking for his mate.

"Man, now I'm focused on finding my mate and you know that. I'm tired of chasing skirts because that only leads to drama," I replied as we pulled out my driveway followed by the other two cars following us.

"Alex, I understand where you're coming from. We all want to find our mates, but there isn't any harm in looking," my other best friend, Brian Cullen joked from the backseat. Now Brian was more laid back and just went with the flow.

All three of us grew up together from diapers and have had each other's back no matter what since then.

"I'll admit that I'm interested in seeing what the girls are working with, but most of all I hope I find my mate," I replied as we pulled into the school parking lot.

"What do you know about the Redstone Pack?" Jacob asked as we got out of my car and was greeted with eye winks and smiles from the girls and hard stares from the dudes that were standing in the parking lot.

"I've met with the Alpha and his two sons. The oldest son, Keith is the Alpha to be, and the youngest son's name is Travis. I was told we wouldn't have any problems at this school, but if anyone does give any of you any grief, let me know," I suggested as my pack and I walked through the front doors of the school, heading to the office to get our schedules. As we walked down the hall, we continued getting stares, but I guess we did look a little intimidating. Just imagine seeing a group of fifteen teenagers, with a mix of tall muscular guys and girls with curvy toned bodies.

After getting our schedules, we headed to our lockers, which were all close together. When we were walking down the hallway, a tall dark-skinned dude bumped into me.

"Excuse you, man!" I yelled as I pushed the dude from me, and instantly my pack was behind me.

"Excuse you! You need to watch where the fuck you are going," the chump yelled at me, and instantly my pack started growling, but I had to keep the peace as the alpha, but my wolf wanted to rip his head off.

"Man, I'm going to give you five seconds to get out of my face, before I fuck you up," I yelled pushing the dude up against a locker.

Just before he could reply, the Alpha's youngest son of the Redstone Pack, Travis ran up to us and grabbed the guy, but I was keeping an eye on him.

"I see you still starting shit with people Jason, but since Alex and his pack are my new friends and I don't like your dumb ass, I'm only going to warn you one time. Leave them the fuck alone," Travis said banging the guy against the locker one more time before pushing him down the hall.

Turning toward me, "Man, I apologize on behalf of my pack for his dumb ass," Travis said to me holding his hand out, which I shook in return to show no hard feelings.

"It's cool, who was that chump anyway?" I asked as Travis leaned against my locker.

"That's Jason Patterson, and he thinks he's the shit around here, but he's nothing but a joke," Travis replied.

While Travis was talking, I smelt a tantalizing scent, and when I turned around to find the source, I saw the finest girl I have ever seen in my life and she smelt amazing.

"Mate! Mate! Mate!" my wolf, Evan screamed.

Chapter Three

Jaden's POV:

"Damn, he is fine as hell!"

Standing in front of me was the finest guy I had ever seen, with the prettiest emerald-green eyes. It was as if he had me under a spell and I felt myself being pulled toward him.

"Jaden are you alright?" Keisha asked grabbing my arm and looking at me like I had lost my mind.

Giving myself a mental shake, I look at her, "Yeah, I fine." Feeling that pull again, I looked at my mystery guy and saw that he was still staring at me.

"Girl, I don't know who he is, but he is checking you out," Keisha said drawing me back to our conversation, as she bumped into me and I looked at her.

"Yeah, I wonder who he is," I replied as I looked at him one more time, and then I noticed that my brother was standing with him. "Travis must know him," I said just as Travis looked at me and walked toward us.

"Hi Jaden, it's about time you and Keisha got here, I want you to meet Alex, and Alex, this is my twin sister Jaden and her friend Keisha," Travis said as he put his arm around my shoulders as the mystery guy walked up and stood in front of us. It was something about him that just shouted authority. I'm not sure if it's the way his chest was sticking out, or the way his eyes just spoke to me, but I just felt safe around him.

"It's nice to meet you," Alex said looking at me as if he could see into my soul. Now I know this sounded cheesy, but you had to see that guy to truly understand. He looked just like Shemar Moore off the TV show, Criminal Minds, but Alex was taller. His voice was so deep and smooth; I could have listened to him all day and not get bored.

Feeling someone pinch my arm, I looked to see everyone looking at me like I had lost my mind, except Alex, who had the most gorgeous smile on his face. Then I remembered that he had spoken to me.

Looking back at Alex, "Hello, it nice to meet you too," I replied just as the warning bell rung, and I saw everyone rushing to class, except my group and a bunch of people standing behind Alex.

He must have seen me look behind him because, Alex looked over his shoulder, and then he turned back toward us, "I'm sorry, these are members of my pack and my closest friends."

So, he was the Alpha of the new pack. Damn, they all were fine as hell. Looking at Keisha, I saw her staring at the guy standing beside Alex, and he was staring at her too as if they were the only ones on the planet.

"It's nice to meet you all, but we better get to class before we're late," I said smiling at him one more time, and then I started pulling Keisha down the hall headed to homeroom before she made a scene. As you can already tell, my friend was boy crazy. Now, don't get the wrong impression, Keisha was still a virgin like me, but she was so hooked on finding her mate that she had kissed a lot of frogs, trying to find her prince just like I had. The difference was I was tired of being hurt and decided to wait until mister right walked into my life and Keisha just kept looking.

"What was that about?" I ask her once we were down the hall, and I saw a huge smile on her face as if she had just found a big treasure.

"Jaden, I think I just found my mate," Keisha said smiling as she bumped her shoulder against mine as we walked down the hall.

"How do you know? You didn't even speak to each other," I asked just as we walked into Mr. Walker's homeroom class, and then walked to the back of the room and took a seat in two seats that were side by side.

"I know you heard all the stories of when you find your mate, you will feel a strong connection when you look into each other's eyes. Also, when you two touch, you'll feel a tingling sensation run throughout your body. As we walked away, my wolf was screaming at me to go back to him," Keisha replied as she turned in her desk to face me.

The more she talked, the more it felt as if she was talking about me and Alex because when I looked into his eyes, my wolf was going crazy and wanted to be closer to him. Then I found out he was the Alpha of the Blue Moon Pack.

"Jaden, have you been listening to me? "Keisha asked hitting my arm and drawing my attention from my thoughts.

Grabbing my arm, "Ouch girl, and yes I heard you! If you feel he's your mate, then I'll make sure you two meet. Plus, we're having a bonfire tonight at the house, so we can meet the Blue Moon Pack," I said looking up at Mr. Walker, who was sitting at his desk looking over papers, while the students were talking or listening to music with their headphones on.

"We have to look good tonight. I'm coming over to your house, and we can get ready together," Keisha suggested with a big Kool-Aid smile on her face.

"Why don't you just stay at my house after school, that way we don't have to rush? We both know how long it takes you to get ready," I replied just as the bell rung.

"Cool with me! I can wear something of yours anyway," Keisha said smiling as we walked to the front of the class.

"Yeah right! You still have my red Capri pants and red and black halter top, that needs to find its way home," I joked as we walked down the hallway, heading toward our English class. Then some guy bumped into to me, knocking me into someone. Then I felt an electric current shoot up my arm, causing me to jump back and say, "I'm sorry." When I looked up, I realized that it was Alex that I had bumped into.

"Are you alright?" He asked looking at me, then he looked down the hall.

"Yeah, I'm fine," was all I could say because my wolf, Raven yelled, "He's our mate!" And she wanted to be close to him. Needing some space to get my head together, I pulled Keisha down the hall toward our class.

"Girl, what is wrong with you? He is defiantly interested in you," Keisha asked me while looking at me like I had lost my mind. Right then, I felt as if my thoughts were being pulled in a million different directions.

Raven was going crazy, wanting to go back to him. My heart-felt as if it was finally whole when I was close to him.

Then it felt as if it was breaking into a million pieces when I walked away from him.

"Keisha, right now I'm just focusing on graduating and going to college. After the mess I went through with Jason, I don't have time for any more drama with another guy," I said as we walked into our class and went to our seats in the back of the class.

"Whatever you say Jaden, but I know you're interested in him too," Keisha said as she sat down in her seat.

Just as I took my seat, I started tuning her out, as she kept talking about her new mate. A million questions were floating around in my head, "Is he really interested in me? Could he be my mate? Also, are the stories my mom and Keisha told me true about the amazing bond you share with your mate that can't be broken.

Chapter Four

Alex's POV:

"Mate, Mate, I want her!" Evan demanded.

Struggling with my wolf, I looked at the angel standing in front of me. I wanted to take her into my arms and hold her. I knew I sounded like a wuss, but it was as if she brought out the softer side in me. Then I saw Travis walk up to her, and put his arm around her, making me want to rip his arm off, but I hold in the growl that was rising in my chest.

"Hi Jaden, it's about time you and Keisha got here, I want you to meet Alex, and Alex, this is my twin sister Jaden and her friend Keisha," Travis said causing me to relax, but Evan still didn't like his arm on our mate.

"It's nice to meet you," I said keeping my eyes on Jaden's face, and I thought that her name was so pretty. I know it sounded cheesy, but I couldn't get over how beautiful my mate was.

"It's nice to meet you too," Jaden replied, and her voice was so soft and angelic, that I wanted her to keep talking because I could listen to her all day.

As she looked into my eyes, it was as if we were the only ones in the hallway as I smiled at her, then the bell rang. When she looked behind me, I remembered that my pack was standing behind me.

"I'm sorry, these are members of my pack and my closest friends," I said smiling after I looked behind me at my pack. Then I saw Jacob looking at Keisha, and she was staring at him.

"It's nice to meet you all, but we better get to class before we're late," my angel said, and then she rushed down the hall pulling her friend with her. It took everything in me not to run behind her.

"Go after her, our mate is getting away!" Evan growled.

Sighing, "I know, but she's the Alpha's daughter, so we have to take it easy," I told him, but that didn't calm him down at all.

"We better get to class," Jacob and Travis said at the same time.

Then Travis looked at his sister's retreating back, and then at me with a smirk on his face,

"Alright," I agreed, and we started walking down the hall to homeroom, which we all had together.

Walking down the hall, I wondered how I could gain her trust, and how her father and family will take the news of us being mates. Male werewolves were very protective of their family. Then I remembered the bonfire that night at their house, and I realized I could use that opportunity to get to know her and her family. Walking into our class, and walking to the back of the room, I took a seat between Jacob and Brian with Travis sitting in front of us.

"Jacob, what was up with you and Keisha?" I asked drawing everyone's attention.

"Man, I think she's my mate," he replied smiling.

"Congratulations man! I think I found mine too," I said causing Travis to turn around in his seat.

"Alex, who is she? Maybe I can help you out," Travis asked smiling, and I instantly wished I had used our pack link to talk to my pack.

"It's your sister," I replied ready for his reaction, but I wasn't going to deny my mate for anyone.

"Alex, you seem like a cool dude, and my sister is like my other half, so all I'm going to say is don't hurt her," Travis said looking me in my eye, then looked down at the floor out of respect. Normally, I would have taken that as a challenge, but I understood where he was coming from because I would have felt the same way if I had a sister.

"Travis, I would die before I would hurt her," I replied just before the bell rung for us to go to the first period.

Walking out of class into the hallway, I pulled Travis aside, "Man, I want to keep this between us until tonight, so I can talk to your sister and your dad."

Nodding his head, "I understand! Plus, you and my sister can get to know each other tonight," Travis replied as we came to stand in front of our lockers again.

"I appreciate it," I stated just as someone bumped into me, and as I caught them in my arms as they started to fall, I felt sparks shoot up my arms. When I looked down at their face, I realized it was Jaden.

"I'm sorry," she said looking confused.

"Are you alright?" I asked her then I looked down the hall at that puck ass Jason, who had knocked her down. He was standing with his friends smiling at me, making Evan want to rip out his throat for hurting our mate. Plus, I hadn't forgotten that shit from earlier that day.

"I'm fine," Jaden said to me, bringing my eyes back to her, and then she had a wide-eyed expression on her face. Then in the blink of an eye, she was pulling Keisha down the hall.

"She's leaving! Go after her," Evan yelled.

I wanted to chase after her just as much as he did, then I realized that she must have realized that we are mates when we touched. Seeing her walkway, I felt as if half of me was gone.

"You two need to relax, you'll see them at lunch. Plus, don't forget you will see them at the bonfire. You two have something on your hands when it comes to those two, and it's one more to add to their group named Jasmine," Travis said laughing while looking at me and Jacob, which caused us to growl. Then we all started laughing when we realized how lovesick we looked staring after our mates.

Shaking my head, "Let's get to class," I suggested before starting to walk down the hallway, which caused them to laugh harder as they followed me.

Walking down the hall, I saw that puck, Jason, again and I felt my anger consume me. I growled at him, causing my pack to go on alert and circle around me.

"What are you looking at?" Jason asked laughing, and then looked around at his friends as they laughed too.

Before I knew it, I had him pinned up against the wall with my hand around his throat.

"I'm looking at a dead man, if you touch my mate again," I growled lifting him off the ground.

"Alex, he isn't worth it bro," Jacob suggested as he came and stood beside me.

Growling, "You have one more time to cross me and the Moon Goddess herself won't be able to save you punk ass," I yelled in his face as I tightened my grip on his throat, causing him to gag. Then I tossed his ass down the hallway, causing him to land on the floor in a loud thump.

"This is far from over," Jason replied just as his group of friends helped him stand up.

Hearing his reply, I was on the verge of releasing Evan and letting him have his fun with that punk, but I felt a hand on my arm, and when I looked, it was my Beta, Jacob.

"Alex, let it go! We are trying to keep the peace," Jacob stated causing me to take a deep breath as I tried to reign in my anger and get myself under control.

Nodding my head, "You're right!" I replied to Jacob before looking over at Jason, "He just saved your ass, but next time you won't be so lucky," I yelled before turning around and walking down the hallway.

Chapter Five

Jaden's POV:

We had just finished gym class and was headed to the lunchroom to grab a bite to eat. I knew Alex was going to be there and I was nervous as hell to be close to him again. Keisha had harassed me about getting to know Alex, and my head was telling me to stay clear of him, but Raven was despite to get to know him. I knew he was my mate after I thought about all the things I had been told about mates, but I wasn't ready for the possibility of being hurt again.

"Jaden, please tell me you will at least try to be friends with him?" Keisha asked as we got to the entrance of the lunchroom and I could already smell his intoxicating smell.

"Keisha, I will try to be friends with him, but I'm not promising anything more," I replied before opening the door and headed toward the lunch line.

"You need to stop playing hard to get," Keisha joked smiling at me as she bumped into me, making me roll my eyes.

"And you need to stop trying to be a matchmaker," I replied bumping her back.

As we walked in the room, I felt a strong pull that was pulling me to my brother's table. When I looked where we normally sit with my brother and our pack, I saw that they had pushed three tables together and sitting at our table was none other the new superfine Alpha. Just seeing him made Raven go crazy and caused my body to overheat with need. It was funny to feel that way about someone I had just meet. Even with Jason, I didn't feel that need or urgency to be with him. With Jason, I thought I loved him, but I always felt that something was missing. Then I found out that he was cheating on me with Samantha, during our whole two-year relationship, after I caught them in the janitor's closet here at school.

"He is so cute, "Keisha said as we walked out of the line with our cheese pizza, French fries, and juice headed toward our table.

"Who are you talking about?" I asked while looking at Alex as he was laughing at something Travis had said, showing the brightest smile I have ever seen. Then as if he could sense me looking at him, he turned and looked at me with such intensity, my knees became week.

"Alex's friend, my mate," she replied with a big smile on her face.

I heard what she said, but I was focusing on the deliciously fine guy in front of me, as we continued to stare at each other. My palms became sweaty, and my heart rate increased the closer I got to the table. I had a strong need to touch him or I'd go crazy. I guess fate was on my side because the only seat left was right beside him since Keisha sat across from me beside her mate.

"What's up Jaden?" Alex asked turning in his seat to face me.

Hearing that voice caused butterflies to start fluttering in my stomach, and I wanted to get closer to him.

"I'm good, what about you?" I asked finally looking up from my pizza after taking a bite.

"I'm better now that you're here," he replied smiling, causing me to blush. What the hell? I don't blush! As I looked around the table to get my thoughts together, I saw Keisha laughing at something her mate had whispered in her ear.

"That's Jacob, my best friend, and beta," Alex said leaning toward me and whispering in my ear drawing my attention back to him.

"Is he really Keisha's mate?" I asked, wanting to be sure that my girl wasn't going to get hurt. Plus, if anyone would know, it would be the guy's alpha.

"Yes, he is, and he's crazy about her, just like I am about my mate," he replied smiling and making me blush again.

"When did you find your mate?" I asked as I looked into his eyes, and then quickly looked away.

"Today," he replied making my breath catch in my throat.

Taking a deep breath, "What's she like?" I asked looking into his eye and once again they hypnotized me and was pulling me closer to him.

"Well, I don't know much about her yet, but she has the most amazing brown eyes, long curly hair, and a body to die for, but what draws me to her the most is the way she blushes when we look at each other and the way she looks at me as if she can see into my soul," he whispered making my breathing become labored and I started to feel light-headed. At that moment as I looked down at his lips, I wished he would have just kissed me already.

Needing to get my breathing under control, I looked around the table and I saw my brother smiling at me, and I stuck out my tongue at him.

"Very mature Jaden, what are you, like five?" Travis joked cause our table to laugh. Our pack was used to us teasing each other.

"If I'm five, so are you twin brother," I said, and I stuck my tongue out again.

"You guys have to excuse these two because they are always bickering like two kids. Sometimes we must threaten them with a timeout to get them to stop," Keisha joked causing me and Travis to throw French fries at her, and everyone started laughing at us as we started pouting.

"Very funny! Keisha, maybe I should tell Jacob about how you and Jaden got caught kissing boys outside in our tree house," Travis said laughing, causing Alex and Jacob to growl. I was so surprised when I looked at Alex and saw that he had a sad look on his face, but then he covered it up with a smile when he saw I was looking at him.

"For your information Travis, we were ten years old, and we were not kissing. The boys tried to kiss us, and we kicked them where the sun doesn't shine, and then we ran," I said before I stuck my tongue out at him again.

"Since you want to tell so much, why don't you tell everyone about you peeing in the bed until you were nine," Keisha said causing everyone to bust out laughing, and Travis growled at us.

"You two are dead," Travis yelled standing up.

See, my brother can dish it out, but he can't take it as usual. Seeing him get up, I was still laughing as I stood up and grabbed the nearest person to me and quickly pulled them in front of me. That happened to be Alex, and as soon as I touched his arm, a tingle shot up my arms making me gasp. Almost instantly, I found myself wrapped in his muscular arms, as we all laughed at Travis as he chased after Keisha, who was wrapped in Jacobs's arms.

"I will get you two back, and you're not going to know when it's coming," Travis said laughing while giving us the middle finger.

"I'll protect you," Alex whispered in my ear while laughing at us, causing me to blush again and put my face into his chest.

"Thank you," I whispered back enjoying being so close to him that I could hear his heartbeat and feeling the warmth radiating from his amazing body. Then as we looked into each other eyes, the bell rang, and I stepped back from Alex, instantly missing his warmth.

"Isn't this a pretty picture?" Alex and I both looked toward the person speaking, to see it's none other than Jason, my ex, which caused us both to growl.

Chapter Six

Alex's POV:

"I know this punk ass fool isn't talking to us," I said as I looked at Jason while holding Jaden close to me, just in case that fool wanted to start some shit.

"What do you want Jason?" Jaden demanded as she stepped back from me with her hands balled into a fist. Damn, she was turning me on with her feistiness.

"I want to know why you all up in this joker's face?" Jason asked causing Evan to growl as I fought him to keep control, but I pulled Jaden behind me as I step up to this fool.

See the question we're wondering, is why the fuck you always go something to say? See after our earlier run in, I thought you would've got the message, I guess not," I said before I punched his ass in the jaw and he fell to the floor. As I was about to kick his ass, Travis, Brian, and Jacob grabbed me, while the rest of my pack stood around us.

"Alex, calm down! He isn't worth your time man," Travis said as I dragged them with me, as I got closer to Jason, as his friends help him up off the ground. I hadn't been this mad in a long time, but Evan and I weren't taking any disrespect from that asshole, especially not when he's fucking with our mate. Hell no!

"This mutherfucker has a death wish, and I'm going to help him out," I yell at I struggle against my friends until I felt a hand on my chest, and it caused Evan to calm down a little, and when I look down, I realize it was my mate.

"Alex, calm down please, he's not worth it. Let's just go to class, before we're late," Jaden said as she put both her hands on my chest and looked into my eyes. After looking at Jason one last time and growling, I put my arm around Jaden and pulled her to me as I tried to calm down.

"So, the big bad Alpha is going to let a little bitch tell him what to do?" Jason yelled just as Jaden was about to lead me out the cafeteria, but I turned around and was headed back toward him when Travis beat me to him because Jaden was holding my arm. Travis walked up to him and punching him in his other jaw.

"If you ever talk about my sister like that again punk, Alex will be the last of your worries," Travis yelled as a tall caramel skinned girl grabbed Travis's arm before he could punch Jason again.

"Damn, I'm late one day and all hell breaks loose," The girl said smiling as she pulled Travis out of the cafeteria, and we all followed them after giving Jason one more warning growl.

"Jasmine, where have you been? I've been texting you all day," Jaden asked as she went over to her brother, and looked at his hand, making me instantly want to pull her back.

"Yeah, me too," Keisha added, standing beside Jacob, who had his arm around her waist.

"Well, you know how it is when you oversleep. Plus, I didn't think I was missing much, but I guess I was wrong," she said looking at me with a smile on her face, which caused Jaden to growl, as she walked back toward me. I put my arm around her, as everyone stared at her in shock. I felt proud that she was jealous, but there was no need for it, I only had eyes for her and soon she would know it.

"Jaden is there something you want to tell me?" Jasmine asked looking at us, then she looked to my left and it was like she was in a trace. When we looked to see what she was staring at, we realized it was Brian, and he was staring at her too. So, I guess you know what that means.

"Jas, do you have something to tell me?" Jaden asked smiling to bring them out of their trance.

"How about we talk about it later at your house," Jasmine replied blushing when she looked back at Brian, who had a big ass smile on his face.

"Alright, I hate to break this up, but we need to get to class," Travis said as he put an arm around Jasmine's shoulder, instantly making Brian growl.

"Alright man, I get the message," Travis said with his hands in the air as he backed away from her and making us all laugh, as Jasmine walked over to Brian and put her hand on his arm, which seemed to calm him down. I wonder did I look like that when it came to Jaden, all lovesick and shit.

I hated to let Jaden out of my sight, but I knew I was being crazy because I would see her tonight.

"I guess I will see you tonight, at the bonfire," Jaden said to me as she came and stood in front of me with her hands on my chest. Did she know how bad I was fighting Evan not to take her in this damn hallway? Her soft touches and those amazing eyes of hers were driving us crazy.

"Yeah, we'll be there," I replied smiling as I ran my hand down the side of her face, while I enjoyed the feel of her soft skin and her heavenly fragrance.

"Alright, I'll see you later," she said before she looked at my lips as if she was waiting for something. Not wanting to push it, I kissed her on the cheek.

"Alright," I replied smiling, and then Keisha grabbed her hand and pulled her down the hall as she looked back at me and smiled.

"Man, you three have your hands full now, with those three. Lord have mercy," Travis joked looking at me, Jacob, and Brian, causing everyone to laugh.

"You just wait until you met your mate, and we'll see how you act," Brian said, as everyone continued to laugh, but I think I was the only one to see a sad look cross Travis's face.

"Guys, you'll head on to class, I need to ask Travis something about tonight," I suggested after I saw him look at Jack, which was one of my best fighters and cousin, who was also looking at Travis with such intensity, then Jack looked at me.

"I understand, just let me talk to him," I said to Jack through our pack link and he bowed his head and followed the rest down the hall.

After seeing them walk down the hall, I turned to Travis," So when did you know you were gay?"

Chapter Seven

Jaden's POV:

That day was getting crazier and crazier by the minute. When I went to school that day, I was planning to go to college, and start a life away from home. Then I found out my mate was the sexy new alpha that moved to town. My ex-boyfriend was tripping and starting trouble, and then both of my best friends have found their mates in the same pack. At first, I was so confused about Alex, and that whole mate thing, but being near him and talking to him, I felt safe and loved. "How can that be?" I thought just as the bell rung to go home.

"Jaden, are you ready to go, or are you going to keep daydreaming about that fine mate of yours?" Jasmine asked as she stood up followed by Keisha.

"Like you can talk, I saw you both doing the same thing, with big ass smiles on your faces," I said as they bother blushed as I led us out of the class, heading to our lockers.

"Look, don't pull me into your mess, and for your information, I was thinking about Jacob, and I can't believe how much we have in common," Keisha said as she put her bag inside her locker.

"I can't wait until tonight, so I can get to know mine. Do either of you know his name?" Jasmine asked as we walked down the hall toward the front door of the school to meet Travis.

"I think Jacob said his name was Brian, and he's like third in command, with Jacob being the beta," Keisha said as we pushed through the doors and as soon as we walked outside, I spotted Alex leaning against a pretty black Dodge Charger and he was looking at me. My heartbeat was drumming away, as the intensity in his eyes drew me to him.

"I guess they are waiting for us, and look at that damn car," Jasmine said as we neared them.

I had to agree with her, I seemed as if they were watching the door for us because only our mates were looking in our direction. Then I was jerked away from my friends, and when I looked up it was Jason.

"Jason, what the hell do you want?" I yelled jerking my arm from him, and I looked him in his eyes as we stood toe to toe. And in the background, I could hear growling and someone struggling. When I looked to see what was going on, I saw Alex being held back by his pack and mine.

"You have ten seconds before he breaks free and rips your head off," I stated as my anger started to increase, because until that day, Jason hadn't said one word to me in months, but now that the new guy was there, he wanted to play games.

"Why are you all up in his face, when you love me?" he asked as he touched my face, causing me to knock his hand away and push him out of my face.

"Jason, I don't know what the fuck you are doing, but leave me the fuck alone," I yelled as Alex walked up behind me, and he caused me to instantly calm down.

"Jaden, you know you're only trying to make me jealous," Jason said looking at Alex, who was about to step up to him, but I grabbed his arm.

"No Alex, I got this. First, Jason, I never loved you. Secondly, I would rather dry hump a tree before getting back with your dumb ass," I stated before I grabbed Alex hand and started to walk away while enjoying the tingling going up my arm from us touching.

"I'm not done with you bitch," Jason yelled as he grabbed my arm again, but this time Raven took over, and before I knew it, she had punched Jason in the jaw, causing him to fall back onto someone's red car.

Pointing my finger in his face, "If you ever touch me again I will fuck you up," I yelled before I took control again and I felt Alex grab my hand. Then he pulled me behind him, when we heard Jason growl, as he stood up and started to shake.

Before I even knew what was going on Alex had Jason by his throat, and slammed him back on the car, "You must be the dumbest son of a bitch in the world, because I seem to remember telling you if you ever hurt my mate I would kill you."

As I watched Alex, I saw his eye turn pitch black and his claws grew longer, as his breathing became labored. Looking around us, I saw both of our packs standing there watching. Everyone started looking at me as if I could stop him, and I knew I had to try because I didn't want him to do something he would regret. Deep down, I felt Jason deserved everything he was getting.

"Alex, please stop! I know he deserves it, but he's not worth it," I said as I put my hand on his arm, causing him to look at me, which made me jump back when I saw that his wolf was in control.

"Alex, please listen to me, I'm fine. He didn't hurt me, and he won't bother me again, right Jason?" I asked looking at Jason, then back at Alex, as he growled at Jason when he looked at me. Then he slammed Jason's head against the car again.

"Yes, I'll leave her alone," Jason gasped just as Alex tightened his grip on him.

"See Alex, he's going to leave us alone," I said as I walked up to Alex and put my hand on his chest and kissed him. He instantly released Jason and closed me in his arms, while kissing me back. When he kissed me back, it was as if he was breathing life back into my body, and I just couldn't get enough, as I tightened my arms around his neck and we both growled. Then we heard someone clear their throat, causing us to pull apart and look to our left to see our packs smiling at us, making us growl in annoyance

"Jaden, I think you finally got his attention," Jasmine joked making me blush and put my head on Alex's chest and he tightened his arms around me and kissed my forehead.

"Very funny Jas! Keep on and I'll tell Brian how you got your first hickey," I joked then I saw Brian look at her with a smile on his face, as everyone started laughing.

"Alright guys, we better get going if we're going to be ready for the bonfire," Keisha suggested with her arm around Jacob.

Then sensing movement next to us, we all looked at Jason as he stood up, causing Alex and our packs to growl as his friends decided to show up. "Jason, just leave if you don't want to get hurt," Travis said stepping up to him.

"This is far from over," Jason replied before walking off with his friends following him.

"I don't like that dude, and something isn't right with him," Jacob said wrapping an arm around Keisha.

"I know! I was thinking the same thing," Alex's cousin Jack said as he stood by Travis. Then they looked at each other, and I must have been seeing things because when they looked at each other, it was with so much love, then seconds later it was like I had imagined it. I needed to find out what was going on there.

"Alright, I need to be getting home, I will see you later Alex," I said looking up at him as he looked at me with such love and affection in his eye, my breath was caught in my throat.

"Alright, baby be safe and please stay away from Jason," he replied before he kissed me softly on the lips, making Raven go crazy.

"Alright lovebirds, let's go," Jasmine said as she grabbed my arm and pulled me to Keisha's car causing Alex to growl.

"See you later," I shouted before I was pushed into the car as Travis, Keisha, and Jasmine got in the car while laughing at me.

When I looked at Alex, he was looking at me smiling before getting into his own car. That man was to fine for his own good, and I couldn't wait to see him that night. Then I looked at my brother, I remembered I needed to ask him something.

"Travis is there something you want to tell me?" I asked in our pack link causing him to look at me with such a sad look, I wanted to pull him into my arms and hold him.

"Jaden, I was going to tell you later, but I guess I can do it now. I'm gay and I found my mate."

Chapter Eight

Alex's POV:

"I've known since I was little that I was different from the other boys but being the Alpha's son makes I kind of hard to be open about being gay," Travis stated as he leaned against the lockers.

I understand where he was coming from, being an alpha's son wasn't easy. You're always being watched and expected to act and be a certain way. But didn't Travis deserve to be happy too?

"Dude, I understand what you're going through, being an alpha's son myself, but you have to be honest with yourself, Jack, and your family," I said as I placed my hand on his shoulder.

"Alex, I just need time. How did you know he was my mate?" Travis asked looking over at me. It was funny that I had just met him, and I already thought of him as my little brother.

"Travis if you want to, tonight we all can sit down and get everything out in the open, so that way you won't be the only one in the center of attention. As for how I knew he was your mate, well you had the same look I have on my face when I look at your sister," I stated as I started walking down the hall.

"I'll think about it, and did you say my mate's name is Jack?" Travis asked as we walked to gym class.

"Yes, Jack is my cousin and we grew up together after his parents were killed by our uncle, who also killed my dad. Jack and his twin sister Kim were only five when it happened, and we are still looking for my uncle Jerry," I replied as my anger for my uncle started to rise. Every time I think of him, I see red, and just want to get my hands around his throat and squeeze. I know I sound crazy, but that man had taken a lot from me, my mom, cousins, my pack and he deserved to pay, and he will one day soon.

"Alex, I'm sorry to hear about your dad, and family," Travis stated just as we walked into the gym to see everyone sitting on the bleachers talking, but the teacher wasn't there, so I guess we got there just in time.

"Thanks, man," I replied as we sat down between Jack and Jacob, just as the coach walked in.

****

At the end of the day after walking out of the school, we decided to wait for the girls by my car. While waiting as I sit on the hood of my car, I looked around at our group as they clowned around, and suddenly, I felt a soft hand on my arm and when I looked, it was a fake looking girl with too much makeup, and not enough clothes on to leave much to the imagination.

"Hi, you must be the new Alpha in town. I'm Sam," she said and instantly I felt sick from her touch, so I pushed her away from me and stood up.

"Look, I have a girl, so you can keep moving," I said looking at her with so much disgust that I wished Jaden would hurry up, but then I didn't need any more drama, and this would result in a catfight that I didn't need.

"I saw you all up on Miss Perfect, earlier. Why would you want her when you can have all this?" She asked running her finger down the center of my chest, making me wanted to throw up.

As I stepped back from her, Kim, who was Jake's twin sister stepped up to her, "Look, why don't you leave my cousin alone, before I rearrange that plastic face of yours, or you can wait until his mate gets here and she can handle you," Kim said smiling as I sat back on my car and watched Kim humiliate that girl. Kim was very protective of her family and was also well-trained in martial arts.

"Look, bitch, I don't know who you are, but you need to mind your own fucking business," Sam stated waving her neck and snapping her finger in Kim's face. I know what you're thinking, that I should have stepped in and broken it up, but I had heard what Sam and Jason had done to my mate, and Sam deserved the lesson she was about to learn about messing with something that wasn't hers.

"See, it's fake ass bitches like you that make us real women look bad, always fucking with something that's not yours. My cousin is spoken for and if I so much as see you looking at him, I will break that fake nose of yours. Do I make myself clear?" Kim asked as she pushed Sam away from me and got in her face again, as we all started laughing.

"You don't know who you're fucking with, I will make you pay," Sam yelled as she and her fake posse walked off with us still laughing.

"Kim, you are my favorite cousin," I said smiling as I put my arm around her shoulder. To tell the truth she and Jake were the only cousins I hung out with or trusted.

"Hey, I thought I was," Jake joked as he ruffled up Kim's hair as she tried to hit him, while I held her and laughed at them. They always keep me laughing with their jokes, and if it wasn't for them I don't know if I would have ever gotten over my dad's death, but they stood by my mom and me.

"Jake, I'm going to kick your ass," Kim yelled as Jake stepped back from her swinging fist still laughing.

"Alright Kim, he was just playing," I said intervening as usual as I hugged her.

"Jake knows I hate it when he plays with my hair, it took me all morning to get it just right," Kim whined, which made us laugh even more. Kim was the baby of the family by six minutes, so I spoiled her a little like I would a little sister if I had one.

"Jake, just apologize," I said because if he didn't there would be bloodshed.

"Fine, I sorry sis," Jake said hugging Kim, who pushed him off her and walked over to Matt, who was her mate and one of my close friends.

"Travis, where are Jaden and the girls? Are they usually this late?" I asked looking at the doors just as my angel walked out the door, looking perfect. Just looking at her, I felt like the luckiest man alive.

Then just as they got to us, that Jason kid grabs her arm and jerks her to him and boy was that the wrong move. Evan and I both growled at the same time and I jumped up and started to go over there when everyone grabbed me.

"Get the fuck off me," I yelled. They must be out their damn minds to try to keep from my mate.

"Alex, calm down and just watch as Jaden handles this," Travis said as they let me go.

Then I heard Jaden tell him, "You have ten seconds before he breaks free and rips your head off."

At that moment I was proud of her for standing up to him, but I was still worried that fool would do something crazy then I would have to kill him.

Then the fool had the nerve to say, "Why you all up in his face when you love me," then he had the balls to touch her face and that was it, his ass was mine.

Just as I walked up behind her, Jaden pushed him and said, "Jason I don't know what the fuck you are doing but leave me the fuck alone." Damn, she was sexy as hell when she was angry.

"Jaden, you know you're only trying to make me jealous," was his reply instantly making me mad as hell that the chump has the balls to talk to my mate like that. That fool had lost his damn mind. Just as I'm about to step up to him, I felt Jaden hand on my arm, making me stop and look into her beautiful eyes.

"No Alex, I got this. First, Jason I never loved you. Secondly, I would rather dry hump a tree before getting back with your dumb ass," she said before she looked at me, then we both looked at Jason. Then she grabbed my hand and we started walking away. As I looked around, I noticed that we had drawn a crowd that had a few humans included, so I knew I had to end that situation quickly or our secret would be exposed. When I looked back at Jason's punk ass, he was shaking and growling at Jaden making me see red.

Evan took over; because to him, Jason was a threat to our mate that had to be dealt with. Evan grabbed Jason by the throat and slammed him on the car behind him, "You must be the dumbest son of a bitch in the world because I seem to remember telling you if you ever hurt my mate I will kill you." To demonstrate we were beyond pissed, Evan extended our claws and as we were about to end that fool's life, I felt a hand on my arm and someone said, "Alex please stop, I know he deserves it, but he's not worth it."

I looked to see who was foolish enough to get between me and my prey, to see my mate jump back from us in fear. Seeing her in fear of us made me fight against Evan for control. I needed to comfort Jaden. Fear was one thing that I never wanted to cause her to feel.

"Alex, please listen to me, I'm fine. He didn't hurt me, and he won't bother me again right Jason?" Jaden asked as I looked at her, then back at Jason to see him searing at Jaden again, and Evan growled and slammed his head against the car again.

Then Jason had the common sense to say, "Yes, I will leave her alone," as he tried to loosen my grip on his throat, which just made me tighten it even more.

"See Alex, he's going to leave us alone," Jaden said drawing my eyes back to her as she walked closer to me and put her hand on my chest and kissed me. Feeling her lips on mine was the best feeling I had ever felt. She was my first kiss, and I'm so glad I waited for her. Letting go of Jason, I wrapped her in my arms and returned the passion she was igniting inside of me as she wrapped her arms around my neck causing us both to growl. Then all too soon, we heard someone clear their throat, causing us to pull apart to see our packs smiling at us, which made us both growl.

"Jaden, I think you finally got his attention," Brian's mate joked, making Jaden blush and put her head against my chest, as I tightened my arms around her and kissed her forehead wishing we were alone.

"Very funny Jas keep on and I will tell Brian how you got your first hickey," Jaden joked making us all laugh as her friend blushed and Brian smiled at her.

"Alright guys, we better get going if we're going to be ready for the bonfire," Keisha said smiling with her and Jacob all hugged up and smiling at each other. I'm glad Jacob found his mate, he was a cool dude that had survived some hard times. His mom had died in childbirth giving birth to him and his dad was killed along with mine in the attack, leaving him alone, but my mom had adopted him also.

Just as we were about to leave, I looked to see Jason was still where I had left him. When we all looked at him, we all growled as he stood up and his group of guys showed up.

"Jason just leave, if you don't want to get hurt," Travis suggested stepping up in Jason's face as I pulled Jaden behind me again.

"This is far from over," Jason yelled before storming off with his flunkies running behind him. I just wish I had five minutes alone with that fool.

"I don't like that dude, something isn't right about him," Jacob said as he pulled Keisha back into his arms.

"I know, I was thinking the same thing," Jack said as he stood beside Travis just as they looked at each other. I hoped they could work things out because my cousin deserved the love only his mate could give him. Plus, Travis seemed like a cool dude.

"Alright, I need to be getting home, I will see you later Alex," Jaden said to me as she looked up at me with the prettiest smile I had ever seen.

"Alright baby be safe and please stay away from Jason," I said before stealing one more kiss. As soon as our lips touched, it was like firecrackers went off in my head and Evan went crazy.

"Alright lovebirds, let's go," Jasmine said as she grabbed Jaden's arm and pulled her toward their car, making me growl. I hated to see her go, but at least I would see her later.

"See you later," Jaden yelled as she was pushed in the car by her friends as we all laughed. Then she looked at me just before I climbed in my car and I smiled at her. Man, I was so whipped, and I had only known her one day, but it felt like I had known her my whole life. Seeing them drive off made Evan became depressed, but I reminded him that we were going to see her later.

"Alex, I got a bad feeling that Jason has something up his sleeve. So, I would keep a close eye on Jaden around him," Kim stated from the back seat as she, Jack and Brian got in the back seat and Jacob and I got in the front seats.

"I'm already ahead of you," I replied as I gunned the engine.

Chapter Nine

Jaden's POV:

"Travis, why didn't you tell me before?" I asked through our pack link as we rode home with Keisha and Jasmine in the front seat talking.

"I didn't know how to tell you I was gay. Then when I saw my mate for the first time today, I realized

I had never seen my brother like that, plus I thought we shared everything with us being twins and best friends. As kids growing up, we were always together, and we were still that way to that day.

"Who's your mate?" I asked as I grabbed his hand and held it in my lap as I smiled at him, which he returned with a smile of his own.

"It's Alex's cousin Jake," he replied with a big smile on his face, as I jumped on him and hugged him as I kissed his face.

"Are you two alright back there?" Keisha asked as I looked at Travis and he nodded his head.

"Yes, we are, my brother was telling me about his mate," I replied. Just so you know, all of us had been best friends since kindergarten and we would tell each other everything, but that was different.

"Who is she?" Jasmine asked while turning in her seat to face us.

"It's not a she, it's a he," Travis replied looking around the car as I squeezed his hand and smiled at him.

"Travis, I'm going to kick your butt if you have kept secrets from us," Jasmine replied as she hit Travis in the chest.

"Yeah Travis, what's the deal? I thought we were friends," Keisha asked looking at us in the rearview mirror.

"Guys, we are friends, but being the alpha's son and being gay is hard to talk about. Plus, I didn't want you to look at me differently," he replied looking out the window.

"Travis, we have been friends all our lives and nothing is going to change that, you big dummy," Keisha joked as she turned on our street while making us all laugh.

"Alright, tell us who he is?" Jasmine asked as Keisha parked her car in our driveway and then turned around in her seat to face us.

"It's Jake, Alex's cousin," Travis replied smiling.

"Damn, he is fine too. I thought I saw some chemistry between you two when all that mess was going on with Jason," Jasmine said smiling.

"It looks like we are all staying together after all, since all our mates belong to the same pack," I stated as I smiled at everyone. That had been one of my problems with the whole mate thing. Having to move in with a stranger and away from everything and everyone I have ever known, but it turns out that I will have all my best friends and my brother with me.

"Alright, let's go inside and get ready for the party," Keisha suggested as she opened her door and started to get out.

"When are you going to tell the family?" I asked Travis as we walked up the front steps.

"Tonight, before the bonfire. Alex is going to arrange a meeting with our family so that he can let dad know about you two being mates, and so I can tell everyone about me and Jake. Please don't be mad at him for not telling you, but I made him promise not to," Travis said as he put his arm around my shoulder after we walked in the front door, following Keisha and Jasmine as they led the way up the stairs to my room.

"Travis, why would I be mad at Alex, when he is being a good friend to you. Plus, it shows what a great guy he is," I replied as my thoughts flashed to an image of Alex smiling.

"I think we all got lucky in the mate's department," Travis replied as we entered my room and he shut the door.

"Alright, if we don't start getting dressed, we will be late," Keisha said as she walked into my big walk-in closet. I'm not sure if you forgot, but I'm a shopaholic. I have a closet almost as big as my suite full of the latest fashion.

"Alright let the fashion show begin," I yelled, which made everyone laugh as we walked into the closet and started finding clothes, while Travis went to his room to change.

Chapter Ten

Alex's POV:

"How was your first day?" my mom greeted us as we walked into the packhouse.

"It was alright, I met my mate," I replied nonchalantly as I walked into the kitchen smiling.

"What!" my mom shouted after a few minutes of realizing what I had said. Then she came running in the kitchen to find us all sitting at the dining room table smiling at her.

"You rascal! How are you going to say something like that, then walk away," she demanded with her hands on her hips and giving me that famous you in trouble look, making us all start laughing.

"Mom, I'm sorry," I replied as I put on the pup dog face and hugged her, which made my friends and family laugh.

Shaking her head, "Boy, you are so bad," she joked as she swatted me away with the dish towel in her hand, as everyone continued to laugh.

"Alright, tell me about my daughter," she said as we all sat around the dining room table with her on my left and Jacob on my right side, while I sat at the head of the table.

"Well, her name is Jaden and she's the daughter of the Alpha of the Redstone Pack," I replied then watched as the smile on my mom's face spread even bigger.

"From what her mother has told me about her, I would say you have an amazing mate," my mom replied.

"What are you talking about and when did you talk to her mother?" I replied. It never ceases to amaze me how my mom knows about everyone and everything.

"I told you that I met her yesterday while I was out shopping. Plus, we ended up going to lunch today," she replied as if this was an everyday occurrence.

"Mom, what did she say about Jaden?" I asked putting the pup dog face on, which only made her laugh.

"Alright, Ava just was telling me about how smart and independent Jaden is and that she hoped Jaden found someone to cherish her because she has such a giving personality," she replied looking me in the eyes, which meant don't fuck up or you will deal with me.

"Mom, I know that Jaden is a special person and I plan on spending the rest of my life cherishing her. Now, I'm going to get ready for tonight, and you can find out about everyone else's mates," I suggested smiling as I looked at my mom, who had a shocked expression on her face as she looked at everyone at the table.

When I looked at my friends, they all glared at me. You see, my mom treated us all the same and you never hide anything from her.

"You mean to tell me that all of you found your mates and didn't say anything?" She asked as she stood up and put her hands on her hips. Just so you know, a hand on hips wasn't a good thing with my mom and it meant someone was in deep shit.

Taking one last look at my friends and cousins, who looked like a bunch of five-year-olds, who got caught with their hands in the cookie jar, I burst out laughing, which caused everyone to glare at me again including my mom. Not good, I quickly made an exit heading to my room. As I walked up the stairs, I could hear my mom reading them the riot act about not telling her about them finding their mates.

I started to feel guilty about telling on everyone until I heard, "Alex, we are going to make you pay" shouted at me through the pack link from my friends.

That only made me laugh harder as I entered my room, but when I looked at my bed, I stopped in my tracks. Lying on my bed was a picture and a note. Looking around my room, I could sense I was alone, so I picked up the picture and note. The picture was taken that day because it was of me and Jaden in the lunchroom sitting together laughing.

Looking around the room once more, "What the fuck?" I yelled before I sat on my bed and opened the note as my heart rate increased.

"I wonder if your little mate is as good in bed as she looks, nephew."

Reading that note, my blood began to boil, and my wolf began to growl.

"Alex, what time are we leaving?" my mom asked as she walked into my room but stopped short when she saw me.

I couldn't think of anything but killing Jerry, and right then his blood was all I wanted to focus on, but I had to fight my wolf not shift and go look for him for threatening our mate, not to mention killing my dad.

"Everyone get up here now," my mom shout in the pack link as she slowly approached me.

"Alex honey, what's got you so angry?" my mom asked as she stood beside me, and then gasped when she saw the picture.

Looking at me with tears in her eyes, she also read to note as everyone walked into my room.

"Alex, what's going on?" Kim asked as she looked at my mom and me.

"Look at this," I replied showing everyone the picture.

"It was on my bed along with this note," I said as I pass the note to Jack.

As everyone looked at the picture and read the note, I knew what needed to be done.

"Alex, what do you want us to do?" Jacob asked stepping into beta mode.

"I am going to speak with Alpha Griffin, then we are going to get ready to attack Jerry and his fake ass pack," I snapped before heading out my room to make sure my mate was safe.

Chapter Eleven

Jaden's POV:

"Man, I look hot as hell!" I said as I twirled in front of my floor length mirror dressed in my red and black halter top sundress and my black Jimmy Choo sandals with my curly hair up in an updo.

"Alright, Miss Prissy move so I can see myself. You know we all got to look good for our mates," Keisha said as she bum-rushed the mirror and push me out of her way, as she looked at herself dressed in a purple and black tub top sundress with purple Jimmy Choo sandals, and her hair hanging down in spiral curls around her shoulders.

"I don't know about you two, but I look fly for my boo," Jasmine said as she stepped out of my closet wearing my black and navy-blue tub top sundress with my navy-blue Jimmy Choo sandals.

I have all the latest fashion as it comes out in stores. I even have the stores put new stock up for me until I could get there and make my picks. My shopping was so bad, my dad got me a black credit card with an unlimited spending limit.

"Alright, let's find Travis, so we can make our grand entrance," I said as I led them out my room, and headed next door to Travis's room. After knocking twice, the door opened and standing there was my brother dressed in black dress slacks, tan short sleeve silk dress shirt, and black leather dress shoes.

"Damn Travis, if I didn't have a sexy mate, I would try to hook up with you," Jasmine joke as she looped her arm around Travis's arm as I did the same thing to his other arm.

"Well sweet Jas, we're both taken, so you'll just have to fight the temptation," Travis replied as he led us to the staircase with Keisha walking behind us.

As we walk to the stairs, we all looked downstairs to see that a lot of the guest had arrived, but it was one person that caught my attention, and that was my mate. I could pick Alex out of any crowded room and at that moment he looked upset, as he talked with my dad and older brother Keith. Also sensing something's not right, we all looked at each other, then rushed down the stairs to our mates that were standing around my dad.

"Sir, I think we need to discuss this somewhere else," I heard Alex suggest as I came and stood beside him, which made him look at me with those beautiful eyes and gorgeous smile, but I could tell something was wrong by the way he held his body as straight as a board and his eyes had a hint of black in them.

"Is everything alright?" I ask looking at Alex then my dad and Keith.

"Alex, I agree! Let's take this to my study," my dad suggested before he led all of us including my mom and another woman I didn't recognize out the foyer.

As we all piled into my dad's office and took seats on the two sofa's and two wingback chairs in front of his desk, my dad sat in his leather office chair behind his mahogany wood desk.

"Alright Alex, you have the floor," my dad said as he nodded his head toward us. Alex stood up and walked to the center of the room, and then looked at me, then the woman sitting next to my mom.

"Before I get to the problem at hand, I want to introduce my mother Jennifer Jenkins, my cousins Kim and Jake, and my beta, Jacob and my third in command, Brian. Mom, this is Jaden, my mate," He said as he walked toward me and pulled my hand until I was standing beside him. When I looked at his mother, she had tears in her eyes, as she and my mom smiled at each and stood up.

"Jaden, it's so nice to meet you finally, after all the great things your mom and Alex have said about you," Jennifer said as she walked up to me and then suddenly, I'm pulled into her arms for a hug. When we pulled apart and smiled at each other, then my mom hugged me too. "My baby found her mate," she cried causing me to smile.

Can you say embarrassing? Both Jennifer and my mom were smiling at me and Alex as he pulled me back into his arms. Then my dad cleared his throat and we all looked at him.

"Alright Alex, there was something else you had to say?" he asked smiling.

"Before we get to that, I promised Travis I would help him with something," Alex said looking at me then Travis, who had stood up and walked over to where we were standing. I knew what was about to happen, and if things went badly, I was prepared to stand by my brother.

"Alex, I'll tell everyone. Dad and mom, I found my mate today too," Travis stated as I grabbed his hand. When he looked at me, we smiled at each other before we looked back at our parents.

"Alright, who is she?" My mom asked as she jumped up and hugged Travis.

"Mom, that's the thing, it's not a she, it's a he. His name is Jake and he's Alex cousin," Travis confessed. Jake stood up and walked over to Travis and grabbed his hand. It was so quiet, you could hear a pin drop. Then my mom and Jennifer jumped up and hugged Travis and Jake, as I looked at my dad, who still hadn't said anything. As the moms stopped the hugs, everyone looked at my dad, who had stood up and walked around his desk.

"Travis, I'm so glad you found your mate," he said as he hugged my brother, making all the women cry, as we watched father and son hug. I could tell Travis was nervous, but he did the right thing by telling our family instead of hiding it.

As everyone was up laughing and congratulating each other on finding their mates, I looked for my brother Keith and he was making his way to the door. Just before walking out, he looked at me, then at Travis with such a sinister look on his face that a chill ran through my body. Then he walked out of the room, slamming the door behind him, and drawing everyone's eyes toward the door.

"I wonder what's wrong with Keith," I said as Alex pulled me closer to him. Deep down, I knew that Keith had always had a grudge again Travis; I guess it was a guy thing. As you could tell weren't that close, but he was still my brother.

"He'll be alright," my dad said drawing our attention back to him.

"So now that that's all out in the open, what else did you have to tell us about?" my dad asked while looking at Alex. Instantly, everyone in the room became tense, and I looked at Alex and he looked down at me, and I could tell by the stone facial expression on his face, it wasn't good news.

"Everyone here knows about my uncle and how he killed my dad and other family members, and then chased us out of our land. Well today when we got home, I found this laying on my bed," he said as he pulled something from his pocket, then he unfolded it. It was a picture of me and Alex that day at school. Then when I read the note, my knees became weak and the room started spinning. As I started to fall to the ground, I felt a pair of strong arms catch me just before everything went black.

Chapter Twelve

Alex's POV:

"Could today get any more fucked up?" I asked myself as I hold Jaden in my arms after she passed out.

To bring you up to speed, I just told my mate and her family about my crazy ass uncle and what he had done to us. Then I showed everyone the note and picture that was waiting for me on my bed when I went to my room to get ready for the bonfire. I hated that I had to pull them into my family's drama. Then when Jaden looked at the picture and the note, I felt like someone had hit my heart with a sledgehammer. It was like slow motion, one minute she was standing beside me, then her eyes rolled back in her head and her legs buckled. Thank the Goddess, I caught her before she hit the floor.

Laying Jaden gently on the sofa, I looked at her and gently brushed her soft hair out of her face, and I realized how much I loved her already and I wouldn't let my uncle hurt her.

Looking around the room, my mom and Jaden's mom are holding each other and crying. While her dad looked down at her, then he looked up at me.

"Alex, what do you need from me to end this with your uncle, before he tries to hurt my daughter?" he asked drawing everyone's eyes to him.

"James, I don't want to pull you and your pack into our family feud. I just wanted you to know that he knows that Jaden is my mate so that you can protect her while I deal with him." I said as I stood up and faced him.

"Alex, you are a part of our family now, and we will stand by you and your pack," Ava said as she came and stood with her husband.

"Thank you both, but my uncle is evil and will stop at nothing to hurt me or my pack. Like I told you, he's killed my dad, my other uncle, and his wife, plus other members of our pack. Plus, I won't have to find him; he will come here to attack." I stated knowing my uncle's way of thinking.

"Then we will be ready for his ass," Jaden said making us all look at her as she sat up on the couch.

As she started to stand up, I rushed to her side and helped her up. The moment we touched, the tingling sensation that shot through me was so amazing, I knew I had to get that mess straightened out before something happened to that amazing woman who I had come to love.

When we looked into each other's eyes, I could tell she felt it too, by the smile on her face. "Damn, I'm so whipped! This girl has me wrapped around her finger and I love every minute of it," I thought as I continued to look into her eyes.

"Alright, now that I've joined the party again, what are we going to do when he gets here?" Jaden asked looking around the room. Did she really think that I would let her anywhere near my crazy uncle?

"You're not doing anything, but staying out of this," James replied. Damn, he must be reading my mind.

"Dad, I know you want to protect me, but if this involves Alex, then it involves me, and no one is going to hurt my mate," Jaden yelled as her eyes began to get darker and her breathing became labored. Oh shit!

"Jaden baby, look at me. You need to calm down and listen to me. Nothing is going to happen to me or you, but for me to go up against my uncle, I need to know your safe," I said making her look into my eyes as I held her hands.

"Alex, just so you know in the future, I don't like it that you're going into danger either, but I understand why you have to do it. As for me, since I am to be the Luna of your pack, then I will defend it by your side, and we will kick his ass together," she stated, and I knew at that moment there was no need to argue with her. As I had learned with my mother and my cousin Kim when a woman has made up her mind, there was no changing it. Damn, what am I going to do with the three of them together?

"Alright, how about we meet here tomorrow and discuss a battle plan. Tonight, let's just enjoy the bonfire and everyone just keep an eye out for trouble," Ava suggested while looking at her husband, then at her daughter. I guess you can tell she was the peacemaker of the family, but I could also tell that if you mess with her family, I bet she would release those claws.

When I looked a Jaden, she was looking at her parents as they started talking with my mother. Then as if she sensed me looking at her, she looked up at me with those pretty eyes and smiled.

"Are you ready to party?" she asked as she grabbed my hand and lead me to the door.

"As long as I'm with you," I replied with a big ass smile on my face.

"That's so cute," Kim said making me growl at her which only made everyone laugh louder as they followed us out the office.

As I followed Jaden, I couldn't help, but look at her perfect butt as she walked in those sexy heels. Damn, how did I get so lucky?

When we arrived outside with the other guest, James and Ava started the introductions. As the evening progressed, I looked around and spotted Keith standing with that Jason kid from earlier that day, and the way they were looking at Jaden, made the hairs on the back of my neck stand up.

"What the fuck is he doing with that asshole?" I thought to myself as I pulled Jaden closer to me, as she talked to her friends, and she just smiled at me until she looked into my eyes.

"Alex, what's wrong?" She asked pulling my eyes back to her.

"It's nothing, I'm just on edge about my uncle that's all," I replied. Damn, I hated lying to her.

"Alex, everything will be alright," she said smiling up at me with her hands on my chest.

"Alright baby, let's just have fun tonight," I said leading her back to her friends.

As she started talking to her friends again, I looked around for Keith and Jason, but they were gone. "Where in the hell did they go?"

Chapter Thirteen

Jaden's POV:

"If he thinks I believe him, he is crazy," I thought when Alex told me nothing was wrong.

I saw Keith with Jason too. I didn't even know they were friends. Why would my brother be with Jason after the way he treated me?

"Jaden, we're about to leave," Alex said bringing me from my thoughts. When I looked at him, I became so lost in his incredible eyes, I almost forgot he was talking to me.

"Do you have to leave so soon?" I asked as he pulled me into his arms. "Damn, he feels good, I could get use to this," I thought to myself as I put my arms around his neck.

"Yes, it's pretty late. Why don't you and your friends come over to our house tomorrow and hang out? Then we can all ride back here for the meeting tomorrow night with your dad about my uncle?" He asked smiling at me. It should have been illegal to be that fine.

"Alright, let's say around one," I replied looking up at him.

"Alright, see you then beautiful," he replied before pulling me closer until our lips touched, and at that moment, it was like our lips had a mind of their own. His lips felt so soft and it was as if I couldn't get enough of him.

"Alright, let's keep it rated PG for the kids," Travis joked making us pull apart.

I had to put my head on Alex's chest to hide my face, so everyone wouldn't see me blushing. I had got so wrapped up with Alex, that I forgot we were in the middle of a party.

"Shut up Travis," I replied making everyone laugh as they crowded around us.

"Alright, you'll leave my baby alone," Alex said pulling me back into his arms, as I stuck my tongue out at my friends and my brother, who just laughed even harder.

"What's so funny?" My dad asked when he, my mom and Jennifer walked up to our group.

"Nothing, Travis is just being a pain in the butt," I replied sticking my tongue out at him again.

"No, Jaden got caught kissing," Travis replied while wiggling his eyebrows at me. He was going to pay for that. How embarrassing can you get?

"Jennifer, please excuse my children. They act like five-year-olds sometimes," my mom said while giving us that look that said, act like you got some home training or else. Which only made our friends laugh even harder.

"Ava, your kids can't be any worse than the bunch I have to deal with. Between Alex, Kim, Jake, Jacob, and Brian, I have my hands full too," Jennifer replied.

"Mom, we're not that bad," Alex replied giving his mom a cute sad face, which made us laugh.

"Yeah right! Just the other day, while Kim was asleep, you boys put whip cream in her hand, and then made her smack herself, and got whip cream all over my new furniture," Jennifer replied making everyone laugh but Kim. She gave her cousin and brother an evil look. I liked Kim already.

"Aunt Jen, Kim had it coming! She put itching powder in our clothes last week," Jack replied making tears come to my eyes. I was laughing so hard, as I was imaging them running around the house itching.

"Alright, we both have our hands full," my mom stated making the adults laugh at us.

As our parents continued to talk, I looked around to see that the party had ended, and people had started cleaning up and leaving.

"Alright Ava and James, thank you so much for having us over, and Ava, I'll see you tomorrow at the mall for lunch," Jennifer said as she hugged my parents.

"You're welcome here anytime," my dad replied.

"And we'll meet at Macy, and check out that big sale they are having," my mom replied smiling, while my dad looked like he just lost a year's salary. Yeah, my mom loved to shop too.

"That fine, and Jaden, it was nice meeting you," Jennifer said as we hugged.

"It was nice meeting you too," I replied as we stepped apart and smiled at each other.

"Alright Alex, we're headed to the car," she said as everyone followed her, leaving us alone.

Looking up at Alex, I found him staring at me.

"What's wrong?" I asked as I put my arms around his waist and he put his arms around me.

"I just hate leaving you," he replied kissing my forehead.

"I hate that you have to leave too, but I will be with you tomorrow," I replied then I kissed his chin which had a cute little dimple.

"Alright, I better go before my mom gets restless in the car," Alex replied after we heard the horn blow, which made us laugh as we started walking toward his car.

Once we got to the driver side of the car, we kissed, and he got inside.

"See you tomorrow," I said trying to smile, but inside it felt like I was losing him again.

"Alright baby, call me if you need me," he said just before pulling out of our driveway and leaving me there with my brother and friends, who had to say goodbye to their mates too.

"Damn, I hate they had to leave," Jasmine grumbled as she hugged me.

"Me too," I replied as we watched their car's tail lights as it disappeared.

"Alright, this calls for a night of ice cream, chips, and cookies in front of the big screen TV, watching chick flicks until we pass out," Travis suggested while hugging all of us, and making us laugh as we headed inside to start our movie night.

As we raided the kitchen, my thoughts went back to Keith and Jason. I was trying to figure out what was up with those two, and why wasn't Keith at the party most of the time since he was about to be the alpha of the pack?

Chapter Fourteen

Jaden's POV:

"Damn, I can't get any sleep," I said to myself as I looked over at Keisha, who had her mouth wide open and snoring. Keisha was a lightweight when it came to drinking, and she had a few cocktails at the party.

Since I couldn't get any sleep, I thought that I may as well go get me something to drink, and then go sleep with Travis, and I'll let Jasmine and Keisha have my room. As I walked down the stairs, I noticed that the patio door was open, and as I got closer to the door, I could hear Keith's voice.

"I can't wait until this is done, so I can have this pack to myself, without the old man around," he said, and I could feel my anger start to rise as he spoke of our father that way.

"Man, just be patient! Just think in a couple of days, you will have this pack and I will have Alex's pack after we kill them both," said another voice that I recognized as Jason's. Those fools were crazy if they thought they were going to kill my dad and Alex.

"What are we going to do about Jaden and Travis?" Keith asked. I tried to look out the door without being seen, but all I saw was their shadow from the area light outside.

"Well, as for Jaden, I plan to make her my wife whether she likes it or not. As for Travis, I say we kill his gay ass too, so he doesn't cause us any more trouble," Jason said as my body started to shake from anger. The nerve of those two assholes thinking they can just kill my family, and take what they want, well they have another thing coming.

"That sounds like a plan! I never liked his punk ass anyway and as for my spoiled ass sister, she's all yours,"

Keith stated laughing. Damn, I know we weren't close, but I didn't think he hated us that much. It was making me sick to the stomach to hear my brother planning to kill my dad, my mate, and our brother, then sell me to my worst enemy. That was fucked up on so many all levels.

"What about your mom? You know she will be a problem too," Jason stated.

"We will make it seem like an accident and kill my parents together," Keith stated as if it was an everyday occurrence. Those fools were crazy, and I had to warn my dad and Alex.

Maybe I could sneak out and worn Alex, then bring him back there to warn my dad together. Being as quiet as I could, I turned around and walked to the front door and eased outside. I knew if I tried to turn on my car, they would hear me. So, I decided to shift and run to Alex's house, which was only thirty minutes away.

After I shifted into my black wolf with brown paws, I started running hoping they don't hear me. As I ran I thought of all the crazy shit with Alex's uncle, and then Keith and Jason plotting against us. We needed to come up with a plan quick.

What bothered me the most was how Keith of all people, could think about killing his own family as if we are nothing. It didn't make any sense, because he was going to be the next Alpha anyway, so why go through all this trouble.

As I arrived at Alex house, I was greeted by two wolves, and not wanting to be killed for trespassing, I changed back into my human form.

"I need to see Alex, it's very important. Let him know it's his mate, Jaden," I said, and they instantly lowered their heads, and then turned and lead the way. When we got to the house, Alex and all his friends were outside waiting. I ran into his arms as my tears finally consumed me.

"Jaden baby, what's wrong? Why didn't you call me, I would have come and got you?" Alex asked as he held me, but I couldn't reply. My head was all over the place and I couldn't form a sentence if I wanted to.

"Alex let's get her inside, then maybe she can tell us what's wrong," Kim suggested.

Alex picked me up and carried me into their house to the living room I guess. From the large sectional sofa and big screen TV, I guess that was where they normally hung out.

Alex sat down with me on his lap and he lifted my face. I looked into his amazing eyes, and I started crying even more.

Then Jennifer entered the room, "Jaden, are you alright?" she asked as she started rubbing my back as Alex wiped the tears from my face.

"I don't even know where to start," I said still confused.

"How about I get you something to drink, and then you can tell us what's going on," Jennifer said before walking out the room.

"Jaden did someone hurt you?" Alex asked as he looked over my body for any injuries.

"No. I got out of there before they saw me," I replied as I wiped the last of my tears from my face and Jennifer walked back into the room carrying a glass of juice, which she handed me. After taking a sip, Alex took the glass and set it on the coffee table.

"Alright baby tell us what's going on," Alex said looking into my eyes, and I knew I could trust him.

"After everyone went to bed, and I couldn't get to sleep, so I decided to go downstairs and get something to drink.

Then I noticed the patio doors were open, so I went to close them when I heard Keith and Jason talking. So, I decided to see what they were talking about," I said as my tears started to fall again.

Alex wiped them away and smiled at me when I looked at him, "What were they talking about," Alex asked as he caressed my hand with his thumb as he held it.

"Keith and Jason plan to kill you and my parent so they can have both packs," I said as tears ran down my face.

"Those fools are out their damn mind," Kim shouted as she jumped up and started pacing.

"Jaden, what else did they say?" Jacob asked.

"They also plan to kill Travis and make me marry Jason," I said then Alex started shaking and growling and I knew he was pissed.

"Alex, calm down, you need to be comforting Jaden now," Jennifer said as she put a hand on his shoulder and looked him.

"Alex, we will stop them together, and then we will deal with your uncle," I said as I put my hands on his face and made him look into my eyes. His eyes were so black, and he was shaking so bad, I knew what I had to do. So, I kissed him and instantly his body relaxed, and his arms pulled me closer to his body. Then he growled when I pulled away before we got carried away.

"Alrighty then," Kim joked causing everyone to laugh as I blushed when I looked around the room and everyone was smiling at us including his mother.

"Alright, now that Alex has calmed down, we need a plan before they try to kill my mate," Jake said standing up with his fist balled up.

"Jacob and Brian, you two get everyone in the meeting room in thirty minutes, while I find Jaden some clothes to change into," Alex said as we stood up holding hands.

"Alex, I will bring some clothes to your room for Jaden, "Kim said just before walking out the room.

"Alright, see you in thirty minutes," Alex said before we walked out the room headed up the stairs.

When we got the last door on the right, Alex opened the door. When I walked in, I saw a big king-size bed with black sheets and big flat screen TV hanging on the wall. He also had black bookshelves full of books and a matching desk with papers on it. As I walked around, I could feel

Alex watching me. So, I sat on his bed and looked at him as he leaned against the door watching me.

"Alright, talk to me. I know something is bothering you," I said and as he slowly pushed off the wall and walked toward me, my heart rate increased, and my wolf wanted to be closer to him so bad.

"The only thing that I'm worried about is that you are safe," he said as he pulled me off the bed into his arms. Damn, that felt good and his cologne smelt so damn good, I could've eaten him alive.

"Alex, I'm fine now that I'm here with you," I replied as I put my arms around his neck and kissed his chin, which made him pull me closer to his body, where I could feel his hard muscles flex under his shirt.

"Baby, you scared the hell out of me tonight. When the guards said that you were in the wood alone, my heart almost jumped out of my chest. Then when I saw you, I just wanted to hold you in my arms forever," he said before kissing my lips softly.

"Alex, I'm sorry for scaring you. When I heard them talking, I had to let you know what was going on," I said as I put my head on his chest, while he rubbed my back.

"I'm glad you came here, instead of staying there. After we come up with a plan, you are staying here with me. I can't let you go back there until they are dealt with," Alex said lifting my chin and looking into my eyes. Normally it would have pissed me off to be told what to do, but with everything going on, I don't want to be away from him either.

"Alright, that's fine with me, but don't think you will always get your way," I said as I softly punching him in the stomach.

"Believe me I know! Why don't you go take a shower and relax, and I'll get your clothes from Kim?" Alex asked before kissing my forehead.

"Alright, after running through the woods, I do feel a little dirty," I replied as he led me to a door that I'm guessing lead to the bathroom. When he opened the door, I was amazed to see a bathroom bigger than mine. He had his and her sinks, a big Jacuzzi tub, and a separate shower.

"So, enjoy your shower, and I'll be waiting for you when you get out," he said before kissing me softly on the lips and walking out the bathroom, shutting the door behind him.

As I started undressing, I thought about Keith and Jason, and my anger escalated as I thought of the betrayal and the hurt they are going to cause my family and pack. As I stepped into the shower, I began to wonder how we were going to stop them.

Chapter Fifteen

Alex's POV:

"Those mutherfuckers are dead," I thought to myself as I sat on the bed waiting for Jaden to come out of the bathroom after she showered and got dressed in the clothes Kim had lent her.

How can a son even think of killing his parents? The people who had loved and protected you all your life. It didn't make any sense to me, especially since he was going to become the Alpha anyway. Keith's plans for his brother and sister was even worst. At the bonfire, I had picked up on his dislike for Travis, after Travis made his announcement about his mate being my cousin Jake and him being gay, but I didn't think it went as far as to kill Travis. To make matters worse, the asshole wanted my mate to marry that puck ass, Jason.

They both will pay because no one was going to hurt my mate and her family. When I saw Jaden walk out of the woods in her pink pajama boy shorts and a tank top, at first my hormones got the best of me. Then when I looked into her eyes and saw fear and anger, I wanted the blood of the person that had hurt her. When she started crying, all I could think about was holding her and keeping her safe. I don't know what I would do if she was hurt or even worst taken from me.

The more I think about Jaden with Jason against her will, the more I wanted to hunt those pucks down and rip out their throats.

"Alex, are you alright?" Jaden asked out of nowhere drawing me from my thoughts. When I looked at her dressed in those blue jeans that showed all her sexy curves, paired with a tight t-shirt, Evan started going crazy and wanted to finish the mating process.

"Yeah, I'm fine," I replied as I pulled my eyes away from her body, to her beautiful eyes, as she smiled at me. She must have caught me looking at her body.

"Alright, you're fine. I'll let it go for now," she replied as she stood between my legs and put her arms around my neck. Damn, she was driving me crazy and I'm trying to fight Evan as he tried to take over and have her right there.

"Thank you, we need to head downstairs for the meeting," I replied needing to think about something else besides my sexy mate.

"OK, but first, I want you to promise me that you won't do anything crazy and try to deal with Keith and Jason by yourself," She stated looking into my eyes. Deep down I knew that I couldn't keep that promise.

"Baby, I promise that I will protect you with my life. So, I promise to do what needs to be done to keep you safe," I replied as I stood up and pulled her into my arms, and just cherished the feeling of her body next to mine.

"Alex, I understand what you're saying because I feel the same way about you. I just don't want to lose you," she replied as tears started rolling down her face making my heart ache from seeing her so sad.

"Jaden, you're not going to lose me, no matter what Keith and Jason have planned. We will figure this mess out, and then we can start our life together, " I replied before kissing her softly on the lips.

As we kissed, I relished the amazing flavor on her lips, and I felt as if I couldn't get enough of her. Needing more, I grabbed both of my hands full of her butt and pulled her closer to my body, which caused both of us to moan. The more we kissed, the harder my member became, until it was almost painful in the confines of my jeans. Just when I was about to lay her on the bed and ravish her body, the bedroom door opened, and my cousins walked in as usual, unannounced.

"We are so sorry, we just wanted to let you know that everyone is here for the meeting," Kim stated as she looked at us with a sly smile on her face, which made Jaden blush as she smiled too. Damn, how can she turn me on just blushing? I'm so whipped.

"Kim, it's alright. We were just heading downstairs anyway," Jaden replied as she stepped back from me and grabbed my hand.

"Sure, you were," Jake joked making everyone laugh as Jaden started blushing again.

"Alright leave her alone, and let's head downstairs," I stated and as they started walking out the bedroom, but I pulled Jaden to me.

"Baby, I want to let everyone know that you're my mate and their new Luna," I said looking into her eyes to see if there was any fear there.

"Alex, I would be honored for them to know that I'm your mate. Plus, I know that I will make a good Luna to our pack because I will have you by my side," she replied making my heart sing with joy as I listened to her with so much pride and love.

Wow, did I just say the L word? Yes, I did, and to be honest I did love her very much. Man, I never thought I would feel that way about anyone, but when I saw her, all I could think about was loving her and making her happy for the rest of our lives.

"Jaden, you just made me the happiest man alive, and I know we just met, but I love you already," I replied needing her to know how I felt.

"Alex, I feel the same way about you. When you left my parent's home tonight, I felt like I was losing you all over again and I don't want to feel that way ever again," she replied as she put her arms around my waist and hugged me.

"Baby, I know how you felt because I felt the same way. We will work everything out, so we can spend the rest of our lives together alright," I stated as I hugged her back and kissed her forehead.

"Alright, we better head downstairs before Kim comes back," she said looking up at me smiling.

"You're right," I replied as I smiled at her before I grabbed her hand and we started walking down the hall.

When we arrived downstairs, everyone stopped talking and looked at us. Looking at Jaden one last time and seeing her smile at me and nod her head, I turned to our pack and said, "Everyone I want you to meet my mate and your new Luna, Jaden Griffin."

Chapter Sixteen

Jaden's POV:

When Alex announced that I was his mate, so many things went through my mind. Will they accept me? Will I be a good Luna for the pack? As if he can sense my nervousness, Alex gently squeezed my hand and smiles that gorgeous smile that made my knees weak.

"Alright, Jaden get your thoughts off the fine alpha and back to the matter at hand," I thought to myself as I turned and faced the group before us.

"I called everyone here tonight because we have a problem that involves us as well as you. Jaden's brother and his friend plan to kill me and Alpha Griffin, then take over our packs. So, we need to come up with a plan to deal with this situation. Plus, there is one more situation that needs to be dealt with. As you all know, Jerry has made all our lives a living hell, well yesterday he left me a gift on my bed." Alex said before taking a deep breath.

As I listened to him and looked at our pack, I finally realized all the pain that man had caused them and what made it even worst was that Jerry was family. What could have happened to make him hate his own family so much that he would try to kill them?

"On my bed was a note and a picture of me and Jaden at school after we met. The note was basically telling me that he knew about Jaden being my mate and he was going to use her to hurt me," Alex continued as I looked at him and saw the pain in his eyes, and it broke my heart. Needing to comfort him and our pack, I put my arm around Alex's waist and smiled up at him when he looked at me and smiled.

"Everyone, I can't begin to imagine what you all have been through because of this man, but what I can say is that he will not hurt you anymore. You are not alone anymore, my father and all the surrounding packs, which are my uncles will aid us in getting rid of him," I said as I looked at everyone, then back at Alex, who just smiled at me.

"Later today, I will be meeting with Alpha Griffin to come up with a battle plan for when Jerry tries to get to Jaden or tries to attack us. I want us to be ready for anything. So, starting today, we will always have patrols on our borders and we will start fight training today, which I want Jake and Jacob to oversee," Alex said looking at Jacob and Jake, who was standing to the left of us and who also bowed their heads in agreement.

"Everyone, we know this is a lot to take in at once, but we want you to know what's going on, so you will be prepared. Tomorrow, we want everyone to come with us to my parent's home so that you can get to know each other like Alex did last night with my father. Then we can all sit down and come up with a plan of attack. We can even have dinner after the meeting, to get better acquainted with each other," I said smiling at everyone hoping to release some of the tension in the room. I could sense everyone's fear of another attack, and I will be damned if my pack would continue to live in fear of that asshole.

"Alright everyone, I know it's three in the morning and everyone is tired. So, later today you can talk with Jaden and she can get to know you when we will all go to Alpha Griffin's. So, everyone is dismissed," Alex said then as everyone started to leave, Jennifer and Kim walked up to us followed by Jacob, Jake, and Brian.

"Alex, can we all meet in your office for a minute? We have been talking and I think we have come up with a plan to take care of one of our problems," Kim said smiling. From what Alex has told me about his cousins, Kim is the thinker of the pair, while Jack is the muscle and peacemaker. As I looked at them together, I was glad Alex had such a good support system behind him through all that craziness.

"Alright, let's go," Alex replied before grabbing a hold of my hand, and then started to lead us out of the room.

As we walked down the hall, I looked up at Alex and started to think about our life together after all the drama was dealt with. Even though we had just met, I felt as if I had known him my whole life, and I was glad the goddess blessed me with such a caring and strong mate.

Walking into his office, I looked around at the bookshelves full of books, the leather sofa, and love seat, his big mahogany desk with a masculine black office chair and all the electronics. That room was all Alex, and I could tell that it was his private getaway. Alex led me behind his desk and after he sat down, he pulled me into his lap.

"Alright, what did you come up with?" Alex asked after everyone sat down.

"Well, Keith probably knows about the meeting we are supposed to have tomorrow, but what they don't expect is for you to bring the pack with you. So, what we were thinking is that Jaden goes and tell her family what's going on to give them a heads up. Plus, Keith and Jason don't know that she knows their plans, and when we all meet, we call them out in front of both packs," Jacob suggested looking at us and I could feel the fear and anger rolling off Alex.

"Alex, I think it's a good plan, and they won't know what hit them until it was too late," I said looking at Alex.

"I don't like the fact of you going back there alone," Alex said looking at me and I could understand his feeling, but it was the only way, and I had to get him to see that.

"It's a great plan and if you want, I can go with her," Kim replied.

"Alex, they're right. It's the only way this is going to work," I stated making him look at me. "Everything will be fine, plus Kim will be with me."

Sighing and shaking his head, "Alright, I know when I'm outnumbered, but Jaden promise me that you will be careful. I don't want you alone with either of them," Alex replied before I kissed him softly on the lips.

"Alright, for this to work, I need to get back before everyone wakes up. Plus, I need the opportunity to get my parents alone, so we can talk," I stated as I stood up with Alex following my lead.

"Jaden, I will meet you in the kitchen, so you two can talk," Kim said before she and everyone else stood up and started walking out of the office.

Alone at last, I turned and faced Alex, and I found him staring at me.

"Why are you staring at me like that?" I ask as I put my arms around his waist.

"I just realized what an amazing woman you are," he replied as he pulled me into his arms.

"And don't you forget it, mister," I joked as a stood on my toes and kissed him.

Feeling his lips against mine was the most amazing feeling in the world, too bad I needed to be getting home.

"Alright, I need to be leaving, and you need to get some rest," I said as I grabbed his hand and lead him out the office.

"Baby, promise me that you will be careful," he pleaded as I pulled him along.

"Alex, I will be fine. Plus, Kim will be with me, so stop worrying," I said as we came to the front door and he pulled me into his arms. If he kept that up, I would never want to leave.

"Jaden, I know you're fine, but I want you to be careful," he joked. I rolled my eyes at that corny joke, but it was kind of cute.

"I will be careful, now I have to go," I said as the group walked into the foyer smiling at us.

"Jaden, you ready? Before my cousin changes his mind and locks you away," Kim asked before she grabbed my hand and pulled me out the door. When I looked back at

Alex, he had an expression of a sad pup on his face, as if someone had taken his favorite toy, which made us all laugh.

As I followed Kim into the woods heading to my house, I began to wonder how everything would go later today.

Alex's POV:

As I watched Jaden leave with Kim, I felt something isn't right, but I just couldn't put my finger on what it was.

"Alright Alex, what's bothering you other than your mate leaving?" Jake asked as we walked back inside the house.

"I don't know what it is, but I have a bad feeling something bad is about to happen," I replied as I walked into the living room and sat down on the sofa. My thoughts are all over the place, and then add the bad feeling to the mix, I felt like I was going crazy.

"Alex, you need to listen to your feeling and be on guard for whatever it is, because the last time you had that feeling, Jerry attacked us and killed our parents and your dad," Jacob stated sitting beside me.

"Yeah I remember," I replied as that day came back to me.

We were having a party to celebrate my parents' twentieth anniversary and all day I had told my parents and family that something wasn't right and something bad was going to happen, but everyone said I was being silly. Then that night after the party started, we were ambushed, and it finally came down to my uncle and two other rogues killing my dad. Just as our allies came to help us, Jerry and his pack took off, leaving us with the dead bodies of our loved ones to deal with. To that day, that scene still haunted my dreams.

"Alex, we will get this mess straightened out," my mom said as she kissed my forehead and turned to head out of the room.

"I know mom," I replied just as she got to the door and looked back at me, then she headed out the room.

"Right now, let's focus on dealing with Jaden's brother and his friend. Then we can focus on Jerry, so we can finally end this for good," Brian stated from his seat on the other side of Jacob.

"You're right! We need to deal with one thing at a time, and to do that we need some rest," I stated as I stood up and stretched out my arms, and then I walked toward the doorway.

"Alright, get some sleep and we'll meet in a few hours," Jacob said just as I made it to the door.

"Cool," I replied before I continued to the kitchen to get something to drink.

As I walked to the kitchen, that bad feel got worst and as I entered the kitchen I found a pool of blood on the floor, and the back door open with blood splattered on it. As fear started to rise in me, I sniffed the room and I smelt my mom's scent and someone else's that I didn't recognize.

"Everyone get in the kitchen now," I shouted through the pack link as I continued to look around the kitchen, then out the door. It was as if her scent had disappeared, once I stepped out the back door.

"Maybe she cut herself and ran upstairs," I thought to myself as Jacob, Jake and Brian ran into the kitchen.

"What the hell happened in here?" Jake asked as they looked around the room.

"I don't know, but we need to find my mom," I replied as I took off running upstairs to my mom's room.

As I ran upstairs, I prayed that my mom was alright and that she just cut her hand or something. When I got to her room the door was open, and when I walked in, I instantly knew that she wasn't there. After checking the bathroom and her closet, I knew someone had taken my mom. It was like my legs had turned into jelly instantly because I fell to the floor as tears of fear and anger consumed me.

"How could this happen? She was just with us in the living room. Damn, she's the only parent I have left. I can't lose her too," I thought as the guys helped me up off the floor onto my mom's bed.

"Alex, we will find Aunt Jennifer," Jake said as he handed me some tissue, while I got my thoughts together.

"He's right! Aunt Jennifer is the only parent some of us have, and we will find her come hell or high water," Jacob stated as we all started looking for any clues about what happened to her.

"We need to go back to the kitchen because I don't think she made up here to her room," Brian said as he headed toward the door.

Following him downstairs, we ran into most of the pack standing in the foyer looking up at us.

"Everyone, my mom has been taken. I want everyone to search the grounds for any clues," I commanded, and everyone headed outside, while we continued toward the kitchen.

Just as we got to the kitchen, laying on the floor was my mom's charm bracelet that I gave her for Mother's Day. As I picked it up, a chill ran down my spine and I knew that I needed to find her soon.

Chapter Eighteen

Jaden's POV:

Walking back into my parents' home, it seemed like everyone was still asleep, so Kim and I quietly walked up the stairs to my room. Just as we got to my bedroom door, it swung open to reveal my parents, my brothers, and my best friends and they all looked pissed.

"What's going on?" I asked like I didn't already know.

"What's going on young lady is you disappeared for hours and didn't tell anyone where you were going in the middle of the night. Do you know how worried we all were?" my mom said as she came forward and hugged me.

"I'm sorry! I couldn't sleep, so I went for a walk and I ran into Kim. She also couldn't sleep, and then we came back here," I replied looking at Kim for assistance.

"We're so sorry! After everything that happened yesterday, I just couldn't sleep either," Kim replied. Thank the Goddess that she came up with something quick because Kevin was watching us like a hawk.

Just being in the same room with him was killing me. I just wanted to strangle his ass, for what he has planned for our family and my mate. Just as I was about to say something, I felt a wave of fear rush through my body, causing me to fall to the ground. What the hell?

"Jaden, what's wrong?" My dad asked as he and Travis helped me off the ground, and on to my bed.

"I don't know, I just felt scared suddenly," I replied then Alex came to mind.

"It's Alex," I yelled as I reached for my cell phone and called him as everyone circled around me.

"Alex, what's wrong," I asked as soon as he answered.

"Jaden, I'm so glad you called. I'm going out of my mind," Alex replied with worry and anger in his voice, something wasn't right.

"Alex, you're scaring me! What's going on?" I asked as I stood up and walked over to Kim, who looked to be focusing on something, then I realized that she was talking to someone in their pack through their link.

"Jaden someone took my mom just after you left. I don't know if it was Jerry or your brother and Jason's punk asses. I got to get her back, she all I have left," Alex replied as his tears consumed him. It hurt my heart to hear him in so much pain. When I looked up and saw Kevin looking at me, my anger reached a new level and before I knew what I was doing, I had Kevin up against the wall by his throat. The phone fell out of my hand, as I used both hands to hold him.

"What the fuck did you and Jason do?" I yelled as my incisors elongated and my claws extended.

"Jaden, what is going on?" My dad asked as he stood beside me with a frown on his face.

"Well, where to start? Your son and Jason plan to kill you and Alex and take your packs. Plus, kill Travis and make me marry Jason," I yelled as I tightened my hold on Kevin's throat as he tried to speak and everyone else gasped.

"Jaden, where did you hear this?" my dad and mom asked at the same time.

"I heard them talking outside last night after everyone went to bed. So, I went to warn Alex," I replied as I loosened my hold a little since he was starting to turn blue in the face.

"Now Jennifer has been taken and Alex doesn't know if his uncle or Kevin had something to do with it," I continued as my anger got the best of me, and I tightened my grip on his throat once again making him gasp for air.

Then I felt a hand on my shoulder and I instantly relaxed. Looking behind me, I saw it was Alex standing behind me. How the hell did he get there so fast? Needing to hold him, I dropped Kevin on the floor and went into Alex's loving arms.

"Baby, are you alright?" Alex asked as he pulled back and looked into my eyes. At that moment I could see the sadness and stress in his eyes, and I was determined to get to the bottom of that mess right then.

"I'm fine! I was questioning my dear brother here and telling my family about his plot to kill you and dad," I replied as we turned to face Kevin.

At that moment, my Uncle Ken, my dad's oldest brother walked into the room, followed by my dad's twin brother Jimmy and my dad's beta Eric. I had forgotten that my uncles were coming that day.

"Alright, what have we just walked into?" Ken asked when they saw Travis holding Kevin. Then as I looked around, I saw that Jake, Brian, and Jacob had come with Alex and were standing by their mates. Kim's mate was holding her as she was crying.

"Ken, let's take this downstairs to the meeting room. Eric, I want you and two others to bring Jason to the meeting room now," My dad stated as he looked at Kevin and if I wasn't ready to kill him myself, I would have felt sorry for him.

"Alright let's go," Ken replied as he finally looked at me and saw me holding Alex's hand and wiggled his eyebrows at me.

As we all followed my dad and Travis as they pulled Kevin downstairs, we ran into Eric and two guys dragging

Jason toward us. We all walked into the room and everyone took a seat on the sofas and wingback chairs that circled the room. While the two guards held Kevin and Jason.

"Alright, will someone please tell us what's going on?" Jimmy asked as he sat on the edge of his seat followed by Uncle Ken.

"First, let's make the introductions. Alex Jenkins is the Alpha of the Blue Moon Pack and Jaden's mate. This is my older brother Ken, Alpha of the Moonshine Pack and this is my twin brother Jimmy, Alpha of the Greywolf Pack," My dad stated as he sat down next to my mom on the sofa.

"Why is Kevin being held like a criminal?" Ken asked.

"Well it seems as that my son here plans to kill me, Alex, Travis and I'm guessing Ava too, to get our packs and make Jaden marry Jason," My dad stated.

"Kevin, what in the hell possessed you to think you could get away with this? Plus, the pack was going to be yours anyway," Uncle Ken yelled making me jump a little.

"I wanted it now! Plus, I knew that dad didn't think I should be alpha of our pack and the next in line is Jaden, and if I married her to Jason, that would take care of that. As for Travis, it's embarrassing to have a gay brother, much less an alpha. So, I decided to take him out, so I would be the only person left," Kevin stated.

"Kevin, what I want to know where Jennifer is?" I yelled jumping up and smacked his face.

"Jaden, I don't know what's going, but I didn't have anything to do with this," Jason stated. I had almost forgotten he was even there.

"Jason shut the fuck up! I heard you and my brother plotting this morning," I said as smacked his face also.

"We didn't have anything to do with his mother being taken," Kevin replied drawing my eyes back to him.

"So that means Jerry has her," Alex stated sitting back down on the sofa.

"Baby, we will get her back," I said as I walked over to him and hugged him.

"Eric, take these two down to the interrogation room and lock them up with twenty-four-hour guards of my men because we don't know who else in your pack is working with them. I'm sure my brother will deal with them later," my Uncle Ken said as he narrowed his eyes at the two fools before the guards and Eric grabbed them and started toward the door. As I looked around the room, I could see that my family was suffering badly from the betrayal of my brother, and Alex's family was worried about Jennifer being with Jerry.

"Alright, how are we going to get Jennifer back?" I stated as I stood up and looked around the room because that moment was not the time to have a pity party.

Chapter Nineteen

Alex's POV:

The moment I realized that Jerry really had my mom, it felt like a ton of bricks had fallen on my shoulders. My mom had been through enough with losing her mate and her home, and then she had been kidnapped by the cause of all her unhappiness.

As if she sensed my distress, Jaden put her arms around me as she talked with her family.

"Do we know where they took Jennifer?" James asked as he took a seat beside his wife on the sofa.

"Yes, after two hours of searching, our scouts followed their scents to an abandoned housing development about two hours from here, and it's heavily guarded," I stated as I realized that my family needed me to be strong and to be their leader.

"I'm having my pack get ready to attack as we speak, but I needed to check on Jaden before I left," I stated as I stood up and she wrapped her arms around me.

"Well, since you're my niece's mate, that makes you family and we protect our family. So, if you go to war, then we are too," Ken stated as he also stood up followed by James and Jimmy.

"Alex, we know that your uncle put you and your pack through hell by killing your dad and other family members and not to mention taking away your home. Now, the fool has his sights on our daughter to hurt you. We want to help you because you are a part of our family now," Ava stated as she came and stood in front of me and Jaden. Looking at mother and daughter standing together, I can see where Jaden got most of her features and her strong personality.

"She right! Alex, you're stuck with us," Jimmy stated laughing which we all joined in.

"Now, what's this about your uncle having his eyes on Jaden?" Ken asked drawing us back on topic.

"Yesterday after I met Jaden and we found out we were mates, I found a picture taken of me and Jaden at lunch laying on my bed, along with a note basically telling me he knew about Jaden and that he was going to try to take her away from me," I replied as my anger threaten to overtake me at the thought of Jerry getting his hands on Jaden.

"Well, he fucked up now! Nobody threatens my niece," Jimmy stated as his eyes became darker as if he was fighting his wolf also.

"Alright, I say we head out just before dark and use it to cover us as we attack," James stated as he walked over to a map that was hanging on the wall behind his desk.

"That sounds like a good plan, and that will give us time to call our reinforcements and rest up before leaving," Ken stated.

"Now that we have settled that, everyone head to the dining room for breakfast, and then everyone will rest up," Ava stated before she led the way to the office door and walked out the room.

After everyone left the room, Jaden and I were left alone at last.

"Jaden, what's going through that pretty head of yours? You've been quiet suddenly," I asked as I pulled her into my arms and held her.

"Alex, I don't want to lose you," she replied as tears ran down her face. Damn, my baby had to start crying. Could that day get any worse?

"Baby, we will be back before you know it," I replied as I dried her tears with my thumbs and kissed her on the lips.

"I want to come with you, but I understand that you need to focus, and you can't do that if I'm there. Promise me you will be careful," she asked looking up at me with the puppy dog face. I told you, she had me wrapped around her finger.

"Baby, I will be careful. You're right that I need to focus on getting my mom back and killing Jerry, so we can start our life together," I replied just before I kissed her on her forehead.

"Alright mister, let's go eat! I'm starving and with my friends and Travis eating, there may not be anything left," Jaden joked making me laugh.

"Believe me, I understand! Kim and my guys can put some food away too," I replied as Jaden led me out of the office into the hallway.

As we walked toward the dining room, I prayed my mom was alive and could hold on until we got there.

Chapter Twenty

Jaden's POV:

After we all finished eating, everyone decided to get some rest before the big battle against Alex's uncle. After making sure everyone was alright, Alex and I returned to my room as we continued to hold hands.

"I'm going to take a shower, and you can make yourself comfortable," I said as I closed the bedroom door and face Alex, who had sat down on my bed looking fine as ever.

"Alright baby, hurry back," he replied as he pulled me into his strong and muscular arms.

"I'll be right back, and you better not fall asleep," I stated before I kissed him softly on the lips. Then I stepped out of his arms before I got carried away and messed up the plans I had for us. Looking over my shoulder just before I walked into my bathroom, I saw Alex staring at my ass. So, I gave it a little shake, and then I quickly went into the bathroom and shut the door, but I could hear him laughing on the other side of the door.

As I undressed, I thought about my plans to give Alex my virginity and become fully mated with him. That wasn't what had me so nervous, it was the getting pregnant part. I had dreamed of going to college, but then I met my mate and all that changed. I found myself wondering what our kids would look like, and will I be a good wife and mother.

Stepping into the shower, and as I washed my body, I started imagining what I would look like with our baby growing inside of me and my belly sticking out. Then I thought about Alex, and I knew he would make an excellent father from the way he laughed and played with the younger kids at the bonfire.

After making sure I didn't miss any spots, I stepped out of the shower and wrapped a large fluffy purple towel around me. Then I ran my fingers through my hair, which was still curly from earlier. Just before I opened the bathroom door, I applied some clear lip gloss to my lips. Taking a deep breath, I open the door to find Alex sitting on the bed in his boxers with his back against the headboard watching a basketball game. Which he quickly turned off, when he noticed me standing there in only a towel.

As I walked slowly over to the bed, I also slowly untied my towel. When I reach the bed, I let my towel slowly drop to the floor. As I did all that, I was looking into his eyes with a smile on my face. I watched his eye turn black with lust, but I could also see the love there also, as his eyes glided over my body. I climbed onto the bed and crawled onto his lap, where he then grabbed both hands full of my butt and pulled me closer to his hard manhood. The size of his manhood, had me wondering if he would even fit inside of me.

"Baby, are you sure you ready for this? I don't want to rush you into anything," Alex asked just before he started kissing my neck.

"Alex, I'm ready to be your mate completely and have our babies," I replied as I placed my hands on both sides of his face and kissed him with all the love and desire that was running through my body and soul.

As we continued to kiss, our hands began to explore each other's bodies as if we were memorizing every inch to memory. Feeling his strong hand caressing my breast was making Raven go crazy, and she wanted to take control.

When I wrapped my fingers around his rigid manhood, I was mesmerized by how hard and warm it was and I couldn't take the teasing anymore. I needed to feel him inside me. Rising on my knees, I slowly lowered myself onto him and at first, I felt a sharp pain, but then it passed and was replaced by an amazing feeling of being complete. When it was fully inside me, we both moaned and as I started to move up and down, our wolves took over. As we were enjoying each other bodies and increasing our speed, we both moaned and cried out. Thank the Goddess that my room was soundproof or else, we would have woken everyone up.

Then out of nowhere, Alex flipped us over, so that I was laying on my back and he was on top.

"I love you Jaden," he gasped as he filled me with his manhood and I cried out. He kept hitting a very sensitive spot inside me, and I felt like I was about to explode from all the amazing sensations that were building inside me.

"I love you too," I replied just as Alex bit into my shoulder to mark me as his mate, and then I bit into his shoulder, causing us both to moan as the sensation went up another level, and I wasn't sure I could take any more.

As if he was reading my mind, Alex increased his speed, as our bodies moved as one. The sensation that I was feeling reaches its highest point, and I felt like my heart was going to jump out my chest. Alex must have reached his high point too because he buried his face in my neck as he cried out too.

After a few minutes of kissing and caressing, we laid down with Alex holding me in his arms.

"Alex, I love you so much," I stated before I kissed his dimpled chin, then I laid my head on his smooth chest.

"Baby, I love you too. I also love the pup, we just made together," he replied kissing my forehead.

"Alex, I want to be a good wife and mother, and I know that as long as we are together, we can do anything we want to accomplish," I stated as I looked up into his eyes that were filled with the love he felt for me.

"Baby, we will make great parents and I wouldn't change one thing about you. Jaden, you are perfect in every way," he confessed before he kissed me softly on the lips.

In seconds, we were hot and heavy again, as I climbed on top of him and our hands were exploring each other's bodies again. As we continued, I realized that I was so glad I waited to give my body to my mate, because Alex showed that cherished and loved me whole heartily. For the next few hours, he showed me just how much.

Chapter Twenty-One

Alex's POV:

Watching Jaden sleep so peacefully, seemed to calm my soul and with us being fully mated, I felt so complete and at peace. For the first time, I finally found true love and happiness, and I had to go face the one person that could take it all way.

As I ran my fingers through her soft hair, I tried to memorize every inch of her face as if it was the last time I would ever see her. I knew that going into battle there was a chance that I may not make it back, but I had to end the craziness. If not for my pack to finally be at peace, then for my mate and our pup that was growing inside of Jaden at that moment. As an Alpha, we both knew that when we fully mated that she would get pregnant. Even though Jaden knew that I was going to battle, I was so honored that she wanted to complete the process, knowing that anything could happen while I was fighting my uncle.

I prayed that I made it through that war so that we could start our lives together and raise our pup together. I just hoped that I will be as great of a father to my pups as my dad was to me.

My dad and I were very close, and he taught me so much about being an honorable man and leader, and I could talk to him about anything. When he was killed, I felt like I had lost my father and my best friend at once. Until that day, I find myself thinking about him and questioning myself about how he would handle that situation with Jerry.

"Alex, we need you downstairs now!" Jacob yelled through the pack link.

Instantly I went on full alert," What in the hell could have happened now?" I thought as I eased out of the bed, trying not to wake Jaden. As I got dressed, I feared that whatever it was, it was not good news.

After I finished getting dressed, I took one last look at Jaden, who was still sound asleep, and I thanked the goddess for such a blessing to have her in my life.

"Baby, I promise that this will end today," I said as I kissed her softly on her lips and headed toward the door.

As soon as I opened the door, Jacob and Brian were waiting for me and from the looks on their face, I knew something fucked up had happened.

"Whatever it is just tell me," I said not taking another step.

"Alex, it's Aunt Jennifer and we need you to come to the meeting room," Jacob replied causing my heart to drop to my feet as he led me downstairs.

As we walked toward the meeting room, I could feel the fear and anger rolling off both of them and it started pissing me off that they won't tell me what was going on. In my heart, I feared that they were going to tell me that my mom died, and I didn't know how I would react. Thank the Goddess, Jaden was still asleep and won't see that side of me.

Entering the meeting room, I found Jaden's parents with her mom in tears and the Alpha holding her. Jaden's uncles were there, along with my cousins, and Jack was holding Kim as she cried. Instantly my guard went up and I rushed over to my cousin.

"What is going on?" I yelled making Kim jump and cry harder.

"Alex, I need you to brace yourself, because what you're about to see is very bad," Brian said looking me in my eyes, before looking down at the floor.

Hearing him say that, caused my wolf to stand guard and growl. As I tried to control him, I looked around the room for answers.

"Alex, my guards found this on our borders with your name on it," Alpha Griffin said handing me a large white envelope.

I knew that it was from my uncle, and looking down as I opened the envelope, my heart started to race as I looked inside and pulled out something that looked like pictures. Dropping the envelope, I looked at the pictures and Evan went crazy. It was pictures of my mom in her bra and panties, tied to a chair with her face bruised up, a busted lip, and one of her eyes was swollen shut and blood was everywhere on her body.

As I looked at her face, I felt like I couldn't breath and my tears started to blur my vision. When I looked down at her body, I saw that they had whipped her, because she had deep lash marks and bruises all over her body. Not able to take any more shit, I released a howl from deep in my soul, and let Evan take over. Before I knew what had happened, I had transformed and jumped out the window.

"These mutherfuckers are dead, everyone meet me at our meeting point. I'm going to kill this asshole now" I yelled through the pack link.

"I don't care what it takes, these assholes were going to pay for hurting my family, even if it kills me," I thought to myself as I ran through the forest with great speed.

All I could think about was the look of fear in my mom's eyes and the torture she had gone through. Then the asshole had the fucking nerve to send me some damn pictures.

"Jerry, you want a damn war, well here we come," I thought as I could hear my pack getting close.

Chapter Twenty-Two

Jaden's POV:

"What in the hell is going on?' I yelled as I felt so much pain and anger radiating throughout my body. When I looked around, I didn't see Alex and instantly fear developed in my heart, that something was wrong with him.

Jumping up, I grabbed a pair of jeans, a purple t-shirt, and my tennis shoes before I ran down the stairs. Just as I reached my dad's office, I heard a loud crash and glass breaking.

When I ran into the room, I saw my dad and the guys jumping out the window, but Alex wasn't anywhere to be found.

"What is going on and where is Alex?" I asked my mom, Kim, Keisha, and Jasmine as they stood there in shock.

"Jaden, I don't even know where to start," my mom replied with tears rolling down her face.

Then I spotted something on the floor and when I picked it up, my blood ran cold. Then anger rushed through my body just as fast but was soon changed to fear, when I realized that Alex must have seen these pictures of his mom in such horrific conditions.

"Please tell me, Alex didn't crash through that window after seeing these pictures," I cried as I fell to the floor, as my tears began to fall.

"Jaden, Alex has reached his boiling point, and now he has to handle this problem with his uncle to save his mom. He needs to focus and only you can calm him down enough to think clearly. Try to reach him through your link and calm him down, because if he rushes in there without thinking, he will get killed," Kim stated as she held me while I cried and looked at the pictures.

"She's right Jaden, try to reach him," my mom agreed.

Taking a deep breath, I opened my mind, "Alex baby!"

"Alex, please answer me," I cried with all my strength.

"Jaden, what's wrong?" he replied and every muscle in my body seemed to relax almost instantly.

"Alex, are you alright? That was dumb, I know you're not alright, but I need you to calm down and not rush into war without thinking and getting yourself killed," I pleaded as my tears blinded my vision.

"Baby, I'm fine now that I've run some of my anger off, but I'm still going to kill my uncle for hurting my mom," he replied, and I was proud that he hadn't let his anger cloud his judgment. If it was me, I would have kept going until I saw someone's blood spill, but that's what made him a great Alpha.

"Alex, I love you and promise me you will try to be careful and come home to me in one piece," I cried as Jasmine handed me a tissue.

"Jaden, I promise to be careful and to come home to you and our pup in one piece. I love you too baby. I have to go now, we just reached their compound," Alex said, and my heart dropped into my lap.

"Please be careful," I said just before the connection was severed suddenly.

"Alex, Alex!" I screamed, but I don't get any reply. My body felt like a limp noodle as my family helped me off the floor onto the sofa.

"Jaden is Alex alright?" Kim asked, and I could tell she was worried about her cousin, because she was biting her bottom lip and her hands were very fidgety, so I hugged her.

"He's fine, they just arrived at Jerry's compound, and then our connection was cut," I told them as we each grabbed a bunch of tissue and started drying our faces.

"We have to believe that they will be alright, and while they are gone, we need to get all the first aid stuff together and get rooms ready for the injured when they get back," my mom stated instantly going into Alpha Female mode, and I was grateful for, because it stopped me from worrying about Alex for that moment.

"So, let's stop with the pity party and get to work," Keisha agreed as she followed my mom out of the office, followed by Jasmine, leaving me and Kim alone.

"Jaden, I can't lose any more of my family," Kim cried, and I held her as she cried. She had been through hell, and she may end up losing the rest of her family if things went badly.

"Kim, we are family and I'm here for you if you need me," I said as I dried her tears. Kim came off as a badass, but she loved her family and I couldn't imagine what seeing those pictures did to her.

"Thank you, Jaden! We better go help your mom before she sends out the search party," she said making us both laugh.

"Let's go," I replied as we stood up and exited the office.

My stomach was in knots, and as we walked down the hallway, I prayed for my family and their safety.

Just as we entered the living room, I felt a sharp pain go through my chest, and just as I fell to the floor, I heard my mom scream my name.

Chapter Twenty-Three

Alex's POV:

"That fucker is mine today," I yelled as I ran as fast as my legs would carry me.

As we ran through the forest, all I could see was the fear and anguish on my mom's face in those pictures.

"Alex baby!" I hear through the link, causing me to instantly slow my pace, as I realized it was Jaden. Hearing her angelic voice brought me out of my fog of rage and revenge.

"Alex, please answer me!" Jaden pleaded.

Was she crying? What was wrong with her? Had someone hurt her? Evan was whining and wanted to go back to her.

"Jaden, what's wrong? Why are you crying?" I asked through our link as I could feel the fear and uncertainty coming from her, making me want to turn around and go back to the packhouse and hold her in my arms.

"Please, let her be alright," I prayed as I tried to focus.

"Alex, are you alright? That's a dumb question, of course I know you're not alright, but I need you to calm down and not rush into war without thinking straight, and end up getting yourself killed," Jaden cried causing my heart to ache as I could feel her sorrow and desperation.

I vowed to make Jerry pay for every tear she had shed, because of his punk ass.

"Baby, I'm fine now that I have run off some of my anger, but I'm still going to kill the fucker for hurting my mom," I replied as we started to see the compound, and I signaled for everyone to slow down and stay focused.

"Alex, I love you, and you promise me that you will try to be careful and come home to me in one piece," she cried causing my heart to ache more and Evan to whine again, making me more determined to kill that son of a bitch with a slow and painful death.

"Jaden, I promise to be careful and come home to you and our pup in one piece. I love you too baby! I have to go now, we just reached their compound," I said as we all banded together and saw that the compound was an abandoned farm, and the yard was full of Jerry's army of rogues.

"Please be careful," Jaden replied just as I noticed the army was heading straight for us, causing me to break the link with her.

"Alright everyone get ready because they know that we are here. Keep your eyes open and watch each other's back," I yelled as the other three alpha and I led our packs into battle going full speed.

As I ran, I headed straight for the farmhouse in the middle of the compound, because I knew that was where Jerry and my mom would be. The moment we ran head to head with Jerry's army, I tackled the leader of the group, who was a huge tan wolf with white fur around his eyes.

"Alex, you take that big one, and we will handle the rest. Then you focus on getting to Aunt Jennifer" Jacob said through their link from his position to my left, as he battled two grey wolves.

"Alright, let's do this!" I yelled through the link as I narrowed my vision in on my prey.

I cleared my thoughts of everything, but my objective to save my mom and kill Jerry. As I tackled the wolf to the ground, he quickly flipped me off and had the nerve to wolf smile at me.

"This punk thinks this shit is funny," I thought to myself as we started to circle each other.

Then I heard a loud sound radiate through the sky, just as I felt something hit me in my side, causing me to growl as I fought to stay on my paws while keeping an eye on my opponent. When I looked up, I saw Jerry standing on the porch of the farmhouse, holding a rifle in his hands, smiling at me.

"This fucker shot me, and is gloating about," I growled as I fought the urge to collapse.

"Guys, I just saw Jerry at the farmhouse, but don't think I can reach him since I've been shot in my side," I said as I felt myself getting weaker, as more blood poured out my wound

"Alex, hold on, I'm coming" Jacob yelled through the link, just as I looked up to see my opponent starting to charge at me.

Pulling all my strength and energy together, I waited until he was right on me, and I smacked the shit out of him with my paw and went for his jugular with my teeth. When I had a good grip on him as he tried to fight me, I ripped out his throat. I screamed out in pain when his heavy ass landed on top of me.

"Alex, hold on, we're here," Jacob said as I was forced to transform back into my human form after they lifted his heavy butt off me.

I could feel my body growing tired, but I had to push forward for my pack, my family and my mate. My side felt like it was on fire, and I couldn't catch my breath, as I looked at Jacob, James, and Jaden's uncles as they circled me.

"Alex, I need to see if the bullet went straight through, if not we are going to have to remove it so that you can start to heal," James said as Jimmy and Ken sat me up, causing me to growl as the pain radiated through my body.

I felt my body trying to heal itself slowly, which gave me hope that I could finish this.

"The bullet went clean through, but you have lost a lot of blood, and I don't know if the bullet hit your kidneys or not, so we need to get you back to the doctor can check you out," James stated, causing me to look at him like he done lost his mind.

"I have to find mom and kill Jerry. This shit has to end today, so I can keep everyone I love safe," I yelled as I slowly stand up and jerk a shirt off a dead man lying on the ground. Then I wrapped it around my waist to stop the bleeding. The pain brought tears to my eyes, but my rage fueled my body and mind.

Returning home wasn't an option, without my mom and Jerry being dead.

"Alex, we understand you wanting this over, and to save Aunt Jennifer, but you will bleed to death if you don't heal and rest," Jacob stated just as our packs circled us.

When I looked around, I saw that we had gained control of the compound.

"It's my job to protect you all and that's what I'm going to do. Now we need to storm the house but remember to look for any of Jerry's traps and look out for my mom. Kill anyone else on sight!" I yelled causing everyone to bow their heads out of respect.

"Alex, we will be with you every step of the way. Plus, if you die, my daughter will have our heads on a platter," James joked.

Even with the pain radiating through my body, the mention of my mate brightened my day and reinforced my determination to end Jerry's reigning of terror over us, so I could get back to her and that beautiful smile.

"Alright, let's end this shit once and for all," I yell just before I transform and charge into the house.

Chapter Twenty-Four

Jaden's POV:

Groaning and trying to open my eyes, memories of that day's events came flooding back to me. Tears started to sting my eyes, as I looked around the room and realized I was lying on the sofa in my father's office.

"Baby, are you alright?" My mom asked as she helped me sit up.

Groaning again as I felt like my side was on fire, and I knew it had to be Alex's pain, causing me to cry harder.

"I'm fine, but Alex isn't, and I need to be with him," I yelled as I stood up and wiped my cheek with my hand.

"Jaden, you know that you can't go after him! It's too dangerous!" Keisha replied as she stood beside me.

"She's right! Alex needs to focus on getting his mother back and ending this feud with his uncle, and if you go there he won't be able to focus and may end up getting killed," Jasmine added as she stood on the other side of me.

Taking a deep breath and trying to calm down Raven, who was clawing to get out, when I saw Kim watching me with a look of rage on her face.

Walking up to her, "Kim, what's going on with Alex?"

"Jaden, Alex has been shot, and the bullet went clean through. Even though he is weak from the blood loss, he is still trying to lead the attack. Jack is worried that Alex is losing too much blood, and Alex won't listen to anyone, who has told him that he needs to rest," Kim replied causing my breath to hitch and Raven to growl out of rage.

"I'm going to kill my stubborn mate," I yelled as my hands balled up into a tight fist.

"Jaden, you need to calm down," my mom demanded in her alpha voice, but it didn't affect me anymore now that I was a Luna also.

"How can I calm down when my mate has been shot, and instead of listening to everyone and resting, he is being stubborn as hell and is blinded by his rage and need for revenge," I yelled before racing out of the room to get to my mate.

"Where are you going?" Jasmine asked as they followed me down the hallway.

"I'm going to knock some sense into my mate! He isn't leaving me to raise our pup alone, because he is blinded by revenge," I yelled as I pulled the patio doors open.

"You're pregnant?" My mom asked causing me to pause and turn around to face her.

"Mom, we completed the mating process this morning. So yes, I knew that I would get pregnant, but I didn't care. I want to start a family with Alex, and grow old together, and I will not let him get himself killed," I said as I felt my wolf coming to the surface.

Then I felt a burning sensation in my chest, "Mate, Mate, Mate!" Raven growled causing my breath to hitch again.

"Jaden, Alex has cornered Jerry!" Kim yelled.

Before I knew what was happening, Raven had taken over, and we were running out the door and shifting in midair into my black wolf with brown paws.

"Raven, what are you doing?" I yelled.

"Mate is in trouble! I can feel Evan getting so weak," She whimpered causing me to whimper also.

"If that's the case then speed up, because someone is going to die for hurting our mate," I growled and then I could feel her pushing forward at full speed, as she dodged trees and leaped over fallen limbs.

Looking around us as we followed our mate's scent, I realized that Kim, Keisha, and Jasmine were running beside us.

"Guys, we need to hurry! Alex isn't doing to good and I can't lose him," I said through our link causing Raven to growl.

"We will be there in thirty minutes," Kim replied.

As we continued to run, I wondered how I could talk to Kim through our link. Then I remembered since Alex and I were fully mated, and the pack had accepted me as their Luna, I could talk to them all.

"Alright, let's go help our packs!" I yelled through the link causing the girls to growl loudly in agreement.

Continuing to run through the forest, I tried to reach out to Alex, but he had his link blocked, causing me to growl in annoyance.

"Alex, when I get my hands on you!" I thought, causing my wolf to growl again, showing that she agreed with me.

The closer we got to the battle, I started to pray to the Goddess that she protected my mate and family. I also prayed that she watched over our pup as I fought to save our pack.

Chapter Twenty-Five

Alex's POV:

Knowing that my mom was in that house with that fucker, fueled my determination to end his life even more.

As we neared the front door, "Guys, be careful! He is always setting traps," I warned as I slowed down and started to pay attention to my surroundings.

The pain in my side was almost unbearable, but I was going to keep pushing. When I walked into the front door, the living room looked surprisingly clean and livable. After transforming into my human form, I walked further in the house to the kitchen, and I went on high alert, because it was very quiet, and no one was in sight.

"Everyone spread out and search the house! Remember to be careful, and if you find my mom, let me know," I said before I saw a door to my left.

"We have your back," James replied as he stayed behind me along with Jacob and Jake. Everyone else wandered throughout the house.

Opening the door slowly, I saw that there were some cement stairs that lead to a basement of some type. I looked over my shoulder at the guys, and they nodded their head. Continuing to open the door slowly, I noticed a blinking light to my left and realized it was a trap. Quickly closing the door, and before I could take two steps back or shove the guys out of the way, the door exploded. Sending us flying back against the wall in the kitchen, it felt as if my chest was on fire. Looking down, I saw a piece of wood sticking out my shoulder, and the blast of the explosive burned my chest badly.

Looking behind me, "Are you guys alright?" I asked as I started to pull the wood out my shoulder.

That shit hurt like hell, and I didn't know how much more my body could take. I was losing even more blood. My vision was getting blurred and I was getting weak.

"We're good, how are you doing?" Jake asked as he came and stood beside me, along with James.

"I pulled a piece of debris out my shoulder, and I'm losing more blood. We need to find Jerry quick, while I have the strength to do it," I replied as I tried to stand up.

Helping me stand up, "Alex, you need to rest. We can handle Jerry and get Aunt Jennifer back," Jack suggested as he picked up a towel off the counter and applied it to my shoulder, causing me to wince in pain.

"He's right Alex. You aren't in any shape to go up against Jerry. Let us finish this," Jacob added as he ripped another towel into strips and started to bandage my wound.

As they worked on my wound, my pack came rushing into the room.

"What happened in here?" Ken asked as he looked at me.

"We found one of Jerry's traps and there was an explosion," James replied.

Standing up, as the pain almost blinded me and caused my knees to buckle, "Let's finish this," I commanded.

"Alex, take it easy. I don't want my niece to kill us if something happens to you," Jimmy joked as I started to head back toward what was left of the door.

"I'm going to be fine! Let's finish this so I can get back to my mate," I replied as I slowly started to step over the rubble and headed down the stairs with everyone following me.

When we reached the bottom of the stairs, there was an open area with a table with four chairs laying on their sides from the explosion and a busted flat screen TV laying on the floor. As we walked further into the room, we saw a hallway that led both left and right.

"Ken, Jimmy, and Brian, you guys and some of the pack will go left. While James, Jacob, Jack, the rest of the packs, and I will go to the right. Everyone keep your eyes open and watch each other's back."

"You be careful too!" Jimmy added, and I nodded my head.

Walking down the hallway and looking around, it looked like a prison down there. There were multiple cells with chains and shackles hanging from the walls, and pallets of dirty blankets on the floor. Looking at that, made me wonder what my mother had gone through. When we got to the end of the hall, there was another closed-door, and I signaled for everyone to stop by raising my hand. Looking around for any wires or explosive, I released the breath I was holding when I didn't see any. Looking at my group, I nodded my head toward the door, and put my hand on the doorknob.

Taking a deep breath, I turned the knob and pushed the door open slowly. The sight before me almost brought me to my knees. Standing there with a smile on his face was Jerry, and in front of him was my mom. He had a gun to her head, and she was shaking and crying. The bastard had her tied to a chair like she was in those pictures he had sent me. Seeing her in person, all beaten, and bleeding was ten times worse than seeing those pictures. My anger fueled me to finish that situation, and one way or another, that bastard wasn't leaving out that room alive.

"I see you finally made it nephew," Jerry greeted, acting as if it was an everyday occurrence.

I wanted to rip his throat out, but I had to play it smart if my mom was going to survive.

"I see you're still alive," I replied as I looked around the room, to see that he had three of his rogues in the room with him, but they were no match for my guys.

"I see you have a smart mouth like your dad did, right before I killed him," Jerry replied causing me to growl as I fought Evan from taking control.

"Evan, you have to calm down, or mom could be killed," I said to him and he replied with another growl in my head.

"You are a sick ass mutherfucker to gloat about killing your own brother and family. I don't get what you had against my dad and our pack to terrorize them so much," I replied as I walked further into the room.

"It's time for a history lesson, and then you will understand. You dad wasn't the next in line to be alpha of our pack, I was. Your grandfather took that away from me because he didn't think I was ready or fit to Alpha. Then to make it worse, I was to marry your mom, and the one time her and your dad met, they realized they were mates. She left me for him, and he also became the next alpha. Your father took everything from me, and I was determined to make him pay," Jerry stated as he pushed the gun harder against my mom's head, making her whine and cry harder.

Balling my hands up into fist and trying to control my breathing, "I get you and my dad had a sibling rivalry and all, but that doesn't explain killing him and the rest of our family," I yelled as I walked closer toward them, but Jerry's rogues stepped in front of me.

The moment one of them touched me, something snapped inside me, and I quickly killed him by snapping his neck. Breathing hard and focusing my eyes on my prey, I couldn't believe that everything that had happened, was over him being jealous of my dad.

"Make one more step and she dies, right before your eyes," Jerry warned as he cocked the hammer on the gun back, causing me to put my hands up as a sign of surrender.

"To answer your question, I killed them all, because they supported my dad's decision to pass the pack to your dad, and I vowed to make all of them pay. Starting with your grandfather," Jerry confessed and had the nerve to smile even more.

Narrowing my eyes on him, I couldn't believe what I was hearing. Not only had he killed my dad and other family members, but that fool had also killed his own father. I remembered hearing from my dad, that grandpa was killed during an attack on a neighboring pack. My grandpa had gone to aid them and was killed. To know that was all a lie, pissed me off to no end.

Looking at my mom, she looked me in my eyes and slightly nodded her head. I knew she was about to do something, I just hoped it didn't get her killed.

In a matter of seconds, my mom slammed her head back into Jerry's stomach, causing him to drop the gun from her head. I was on him before he could form a thought, and I slammed him into the wall. I punched him with all the strength I had left and sent his head flying back to the wall, knocking him out cold. Jerry and I both collapsed to the floor, and I felt as if my vision was becoming very dim. My breathing was shallow, and as I looked around me, I saw Jack untying my mom and James was standing over me saying something, but I couldn't recognize what he was saying.

Just as I started to close my eyes, I saw Jaden run into the room. She was beside me in seconds. She was crying and saying something, but I couldn't understand her. Taking one last breath, I closed my eyes and prayed to the Goddess that she watched over my mate and my family.

Chapter Twenty-Six

Jaden's POV:

When we arrived at the compound, it looked like a ghost town, and I prayed my family was ok. After transforming, the girls and I looked for any signs of our family, but all we saw was the dead bodies of rogues.

"Jaden let's take a look inside the house since no one is out here," Kim suggested.

Nodding my head, I lead the way inside the house. When we walked inside, we didn't see anyone until we reached the kitchen. Matt, Kim's mate was standing there.

"I was waiting for you women to arrive. Alex and the rest of the guys have Jerry cornered downstairs. Maybe you can talk some sense into Alex to rest," Matt stated causing my anger for my mate to escalate.

Walking down the stairs after Matt, "Is Alex alright?" I asked as I felt a great amount of pain flow through my body.

"He has a gunshot wound on his side and debris from an explosion went into his shoulder," Matt replied causing me to push past him and run down the hallway where I heard a loud commotion.

I needed to see Alex for myself, as I ran down the hallway and came to an open door. I screamed when I saw Alex and another guy fall to the ground. It was like I was frozen in place, as I watched my dad kneel beside Alex. Then I saw Jack untying Jennifer and she quickly kneeled beside my dad and was talking to Alex too.

Shaking my head as I understood the situation, and needing to get to my mate, I ran into the room to Alex.

"Alex baby, I'm here! Please say something," I pleaded, but he just looked at me as my tears began to pour down my face.

Looking into his eyes, it seemed as if he was looking right through me. I could tell he was slipping away.

"We need to get him to the pack doctor now," I yelled as I looked around the room, to see that Matt and Jacob were fighting with a rogue and ended up snapping his neck.

"I'm right here Jaden," Diana yelled as she came through the crowd and fell to her knees beside me. Diana Smith was the doctor for my dad's pack.

"Please help him!" I cried as I held his hand, and it was ice-cold.

I watched as he looked at me, and a tear rolled down his cheek. He took a deep breath, then he closed his eyes.

"No Alex! Open your eyes babe," I yelled as the doctor continued to work on him.

"Jaden let the doctor work on him," My dad suggested as he pulled me into his arms.

I felt like I was going out my mind as I watched the man I loved fought for his life. Then I heard someone groan, and when we looked over there, a man was getting up from the floor. Jacob and Jack quickly grabbed him.

"What's going on guys?" I asked as I kept an eye on Alex also.

"This is Jerry! The fucker responsible for all this shit," Jack replied as they brought the man in front of me. My anger leave reached an all-time high, to finally be able to see the man who had hurt my mate and his family for so long.

"So, you are my nephew's, sexy mate. You definitely look better in person," Jerry said before laughing.

In a matter of seconds, my claws elongated, and I racked my claws across his chest. I enjoyed watching and hearing him scream out in pain, after all the pain he had caused my mate and his family. Then not able to contain my anger and frustration, I slashed his throat with my claws, sending blood flying everywhere.

The guys let his body fall to the floor and they began wiping Jerry's blood from their face and hands.

"Jaden!" Diana yelled.

When I looked over at Alex, he had transformed into his wolf form. I ran over to them and ran my hand through his fur, and I could see that he was breathing barely.

"Is he alright?" I asked as Raven whimpered in my head.

"I've managed to clean his wounds and was able to get him to shift, so he can heal quicker. We need to get him back to the infirmary, so I can monitor him until he wakes up," Diana replied as she finished packing up her instruments into her bag.

"Thank you for saving my mate," I cried as I hugged her.

"You don't have to thank me. You two are family and we look out for our own," Diana replied as she hugged me back.

Pulling back from her and looking around the room until I saw my dad," Dad, we need to move him now," I stated as I ran my hand through Alex's fur.

"Let's do this," My dad replied before him, my two uncles, Jack, Jacob and Brian lifted Alex off the floor.

As I followed them out of the room, I prayed that my mate made it. I looked to my left and Jennifer was crying as she looked at Alex.

Taking off my shirt, since I had on a sports bra, and I handed it to Jennifer.

"Thank you," she whispered as she pulled the shirt on.

"You're welcome," I replied as I hugged her, and then we continued to follow the guys.

Looking back at Alex, as we finally made it out of the house," He is going to be fine," I whispered as a tear rolled down my cheek.

"Yes, he will," Jennifer added as she wrapped her arm around my shoulder and we watched as they placed Alex onto the back of a pickup truck and Diana and her assistant jumped in the front seat.

"Jaden, you and the girls ride back with Alex, and we will be right behind you," My dad suggested.

"Alright dad," I replied as I climbed into the bed of the truck and sat as close to Alex as I could, and started to rub my fingers through his fur, so he would know I was there.

After we all climbed into the truck, Diana took off. As we made the journey back to the packhouse, I said a silent prayer to the Goddess, asking her to watch over my mate and heal him. I knew that he would fight to stay with us, and his strength and determination was what was driving me to be strong for us both at that moment. I knew he loved me, and nothing was going to stand in his way of coming back to me and our pup.

Epilogue

Alex's POV:

"Alexander Jenkins get your butt down to my office now!" I yelled through the pack link as I shook my head while sitting behind my desk.

Since that fateful day at my uncle's compound, I had made a full recovery and I have continued to lead my pack with my beautiful mate by my side.

Looking at my door as it crept open, I watched as my ten years old son poked his head in my office.

"Yes dad," Alexander Jr said.

"Come in and shut the door," I said as I leaned forward on my desk and folded my arms in front of me.

"Yes dad," he replied.

Looking my son in his eyes, "Do you want to tell me what happened at school today?" I asked him in a stern voice.

Signing, "Dad, Jeremy Wilkins was picking on Jessica, and you told me to protect her and that's why I punched him in his nose," My son replied, and I had to resist the smile that threatened to come to my lips.

Jessica was our eight years old daughter and Alexander took his big brother role very seriously as you could tell.

"Son, I get you were protecting your sister, but next time try talking it out first before you use your fist. As the next Alpha of this pack, you must learn that violence isn't always the answer," I said as I looked at my son, and saw so much of me in him.

Looking down at his hands, and then back up at me, "You're right dad! I'll apologize to him tomorrow at school. I want to be a good Alpha like you," he replied causing pride to swell inside my chest.

"Son, you will make a great Alpha," I said as I walked around my desk and sat on the front of my desk in front of my son.

"Thanks, dad," he replied as he stood up and hugged me.

"Anytime son," I replied as I kissed his forehead, and someone knocked on my office door.

"Come in," I stated, and moments later, Jaden walked into the room, looking gorgeous as ever, and four months pregnant with our third child.

"Hey guys," she greeted as she walked over to us and kissed my son on his forehead, and then kissed me softly on my lips.

I could never get enough of her, and I loved her even more as each day went by.

"Hey, babe, what are you doing out of bed?" I asked as I raised an eyebrow at her.

Smiling, "I heard you calling our baby boy and I wanted to see what he had been up too now," she replied as she looked down at our son and he gave her the puppy dog face, which made me chuckle.

"Jr was protecting his sister and punched Jeremy in the face, but we talked about it and he knows to talk things out first," I stated as I looked down at my son, and he nodded his head in agreement.

"I'm glad you two talked it out. Son, you need to go finish your homework," Jaden suggested as she sat down on the front of my desk beside me and I wrapped my arm around her.

"Yes mom," our son replied before heading out of my office and closing the door behind him.

"He is so much like you," Jaden said as she looked over at me and smiled.

Nodding my head," You are so right, and that's why I know he will be a great man and Alpha. He is so smart, and I can't wait to see the man he becomes," I replied as I pulled her closer to me and kissed her forehead. "Right now, I want to know about you," I continued as I pulled her into my arms and she wrapped her arms around my neck as she stood in front of me.

"I'm feeling fine, and I was tired of laying in our bed alone, so I came downstairs to hang with you," she replied before she kissed me.

Looking into her eyes, I was so thankful that the Goddess blessed me with such an amazing woman. Jaden completed me in more ways than one, and I could never repay her for all the happiness she had brought in my life. As I savored her soft lips against mine, I realized how much happiness she had brought into my pack's life also. After everything that had happened with my uncle, she had brought laughter and happiness back into all our lives. After everything my mother had gone through because of my uncle when she found out that we were having our son, she became the happiest person on the planet.

"Do you know how special you are?" I asked her.

"Yes, I do because you tell me every day. The question is, do you know how special you are?" she asked me.

"I have an idea," I joked, causing her to chuckle and kiss me.

"I'm glad you do! I love you so much," she confessed as she looked into my eyes.

Tightening my arms around her, "I love you too baby," I replied before I kissed her.

"Now that we have confessed our love for each other, I need to tell you that I'm hungry," she joked causing me to laugh and shake my head.

Leave it Jaden to think about food at the oddest times.

Smiling, "Alright, let's go feed you two," I replied as I stood up and grabbed her hand.

"Lead the way," she added causing me to laugh as we walked out of my office.

As we walked through the packhouse, and I realized how peaceful our life had become and how much our family had grown. Keisha and Jacob had welcomed their second child that year, Jasmine and Brian had three children with one on the way, Travis and Jack had decided to adopt one of the orphans in our pack and she was the cutest little girl, and finally, Kim and Matt wear expecting their first child in a couple of months. We had even made new alliances and held celebrations to invite them to our territory as a peace-offering. Jaden was an amazing Alpha Female and the pack loved her. As I thought of the years we had been together, I realized that all my dreams and wishes had been answered and I couldn't have asked for anything better.

About the Author

As a little girl, Leanora always had a notebook, where she could write her dreams and fantasies down. Growing into adulthood, she would read other authors work and say to herself that she wanted to do the same thing of being a published author. At the age of 31, she decided to write her first novel titled The Caress of a Younger Man. Since then, she has followed it by Heavenly Kingdom and started The Voluptuously Curvy and Loving It Series, which focuses on plus size women and the men they love.

Leanora started the series because she wanted to create a movement for plus size women in the world so that they know that they are beautiful and intelligent, and they also deserve a happy ending. In the Voluptuously Curvy and Loving It Series, the books are titled Smooth as Silk, Finding Love Within, His Forgotten Lover, Drafted for Love, and finally Planning for Forever.

Recently, Leanora released a new series titled The Musical Curves Series which starts with Rhymes from the Heart and then Producing Love Together. Throughout the whole process of becoming a published author, Leanora has learned that to write a great novel, she had to be willing to learn and apply the information. She also appreciates all the authors that offered her advice and knowledge.

Author Leanora Moore can be contacted at:

- **Website:** www.leanoramoore.com
- **Facebook:**
  www.facebook.com/leanoramoorem78
- **Twitter:** @leanora_moore
- **Email:** leanoramoore@yahoo.com

Also Get Ready for the Release of: Musical Curves Series:

- **Soothing Her Soul: Volume Four – February 2019**